DEATH OVER DEEP WATER

SIMON NASH

Also available in Perennial Library by Simon Nash:

KILLED BY SCANDAL

DEATH OVER DEEP WATER

SIMON NASH

PERENNIAL LIBRARY
Harper & Row, Publishers
New York, Cambridge, Philadelphia, San Francisco
London, Mexico City, São Paulo, Singapore, Sydney

A hardcover edition of this book was published by Geoffrey Bles in England and by Garland Publishing, Inc., in the United States. It is here reprinted by arrangement with the author.

 For information address Harper & Row, Publishers, Inc., 10 East 53rd Street, New York, N.Y. 10022. Published simultaneously in Canada by Fitzhenry & Whiteside Limited, Toronto.

First PERENNIAL LIBRARY edition published 1985.

Library of Congress Cataloging in Publication Data

Death over deep water.
"Perennial Library."
I. Title.
PR6005.H323D4 1985 823'.914 84-48184
ISBN 0-06-080740-7 (pbk.)

---

85 86 87 88 89 10 9 8 7 6 5 4 3 2 1

DEATH OVER DEEP WATER

— 1 —

The tourists panted up the Sacred Way, in a heat that weighted their cameras and turned clutched guide-books into damp relics. A confusion of voices rose above the dust, telling in many languages of the time when Greece had stood alone in her glory. The Parthenon remained serene, even after the ravages of every race that had broken into the peace of Athens. The party from the British cruise-ship *Inquirer* huddled in a patch of shade, cringing from the sun which they had travelled far to find, and listened to their guide.

Adam Ludlow stood defiantly in the sun on the edge of the group. His tall, gaunt figure was conspicuous in an old tennis-shirt and heavy tweed trousers supported inelegantly by a leather belt. As he had severely remarked to a young colleague who had tried to tell him what clothes to get for the Mediterranean climate, there was no point in buying special things for a fortnight when the rest of the year had to be spent in a country which demanded nothing but the most effective protection against rain and wind. Cheerfully careless of an environment of bare arms and abbreviated shorts, he gazed at the great ruin and was happy in his own meditations.

It had been, he decided, a good plan to avoid the ships that carried their own lecturers and turned the holiday into an educational course. As a university teacher, he heard quite enough of his own lectures during the year without listening to others holding forth when he was supposed to be enjoying himself. Ludlow is inclined to fancy that he can do most things as well as other people if he tries, and his closest friends might have detected a slight jealousy in his invective against classical scholars who got free holidays by giving instruction on cruises. It seemed much better to have days of complete leisure at sea and to depend on the guides of the different countries when one came to them. Such as the plump young Greek woman in a bright yellow dress and a huge straw hat who was now telling them what they should know.

"And here we are seeing the Erectheion, where was standing once the statue of Pallas Athene in wood of the olive tree. Please to note the statues of the Karyatides, old-time maidens who are carrying on their heads the offerings for the goddess..."

Ludlow, who had done his preparatory reading before he came, let the words flow over him while he made up his own pictures of the past. Since he is an observer of human nature, he had a thought also for his fellow-passengers. After three days, they were beginning to sort themselves out into definite personalities, emerging from the faceless and slightly hostile anonymity which cloaks any group of people thrown together in company for the first time. Now Ludlow's grey eyes under their heavy brows were watching the Acton family, or at least the three members of it who could be seen. David Acton was on the other side of the group, still contriving to look exactly like a middle-aged English business-man in spite of his short-sleeved shirt and Bermuda cotton shorts. He had taken off his sunglasses there in the shade and was scratching his nose with them as if he were sizing up the terms of a difficult transaction in his own office. The bald patch on top of his head was concealed now by a smart linen cap. He gazed at antiquity with the same sadness that he seemed to bring to every facet of his life.

His wife Elizabeth was as clearly English as he. It was not so much that she was tall and thin, with an unpowdered face gleaming above a cotton dress that did not hang evenly at the hem. It was rather the expression of concern at being so far from home, the obvious anxiety about whether the food was fit to eat, the frown of regret at not having brought a woolly cardigan in case it got chilly later in the day. So the interesting thing, Ludlow thought, was how on earth David Acton had managed to acquire a sister like Diana and why she should have wanted to come on a holiday with them. Diana Acton was perhaps fifteen years younger than her brother, but the difference between them could not be dismissed as a matter of age alone. The oddness of heredity had given the solid, anxious business-man a sister of a rare and extravagant beauty. As tall as Elizabeth, she carried herself with an easy grace that made people notice her even among the longer-established attractions of the Acropolis. She always contrived to look interested, yet faintly amused, by whatever she was seeing; and she seemed enviably cool in the morning's heat. Her skin was already richly dark, without the transition of angry red through which most of her compatriots were still passing. With her black hair, she seemed as native to the place as the stone girls of the Erectheion; and it seemed too that such beauty must be as permanent as theirs. It was a thought that made Ludlow feel uneasy and strangely troubled: one could not imagine that Diana Acton would ever grow old.

However, it would be a good thing when her niece grew a little older. Theresa Acton, seventeen years old and hating it, had wandered away and was refusing to take any notice either of the guide's discourse or of her mother's frequent anxious jerks of the head. She had climbed to a higher place and stood looking away from the Parthenon to the darker hills inland. She had a beauty of face and figure which a few years would perhaps make perfect; like her aunt Diana, she was going to be most attractive when she was thirty. At present she chose to mar herself by an eccentric make-up that ringed her eyes with blue shadow, made her lips purple and offset it all by a defiantly white face. She reacted like a wild cat to any approach. Not a happy family, Ludlow decided, but held together by some invisible bond of their own.

Ludlow's reverie was broken by a strong American voice, which he had already come to accept as one of the drawbacks which every holiday brings with it. Julie West was not a woman that one could dislike without feeling mean about it. She was full of the friendliness, the spirit of good-neighbourship, the avidity for information, which characterize the American abroad. So much plain human virtue could not be rebuffed, but it could perhaps have been enhanced by realizing that silence can be a virtue as well.

"Oh, Professor Ludlow, can you tell me something?"

Ludlow knows that he is unlikely ever to be a professor and has stopped worrying about it, but he never minds the flattery of being thus wrongly addressed. Also he never minds giving information. He therefore looked down benevolently on the little bespectacled woman, probably about Diana's age but so different in every way, and invited further interrogation.

"You remember that old theatre we saw at that place in Sicily the first day out?"

"Taormina. Yes, indeed I do."

"Well, can you tell me, was that built by the same people who built this temple?"

"No, Miss West. It's of a different period altogether. The Parthenon which we see now was built in the fifth century B.C., in the greatest age of Ancient Greece. The Taormina theatre was considerably later."

"Well, thank you. I guess it's just too confusing trying to sort out all of these different dates and places."

"We have a great deal more to see yet," Ludlow said severely, as if he were exhorting one of his students to greater efforts.

"I know, isn't it wonderful? We haven't got anything as old as this in the States, you know."

"So I believe."

"Have you ever been to our country, Professor Ludlow?"

"No. My travels generally take me south and east." Politeness stopped him from saying that he felt no enthusiasm about visiting America, which he imagined to be even farther than Britain down the decadent path of science and technology.

"You ought to come. We'd sure love to have you lecture to us about all these old Greek and Roman places.

"Classical antiquity is not really my field, Miss West. My own subject is English."

"But you know an awful lot about other things too."

"One reads," Ludlow explained modestly. "There is little enough opportunity for continuing one's education on the derisory salary that the Treasury allows us. And the period humorously known as the Long Vacation soon disappears in a flurry of examining at the beginning and a weariness of preparation at the end. However, the Government has not yet pulled down all the libraries in order to build atomic computers or whatever the latest nonsense may be. The time is rapidly approaching, but at present we are still allowed to have a few books."

Since Julie West did not know Ludlow very well, this typical and unmalicious speech silenced her more effectively than any studied insult. She became very busy with the exposure-meter attached to her camera, and Ludlow was left in peace to enjoy the rest of the morning.

The group moved on, grasping at the wonders of a city which might possibly be understood in a lifetime. Ludlow fretted at the way in which a glimpse of new beauty was given and then wrenched away, but consoled himself with the fact of being away from his desk and the routine of the term. Like many men who love their work, he took pleasure now in picturing it as a miserable grind from which he had temporarily escaped. The holiday pleasure can thus be increased, without the souring undercurrent of truth which spoils it for those who really dislike going back. Being a shy though friendly kind of man, Ludlow had not yet made much contact with the others in the party. He continued to observe the English, ill at ease in not speaking to each other but suspicious of doing so; the Americans, cheerfully extrovert in concealment of a pathetic anxiety to be liked; and the few French and Italian passengers who kept together in their national groups and defied anyone else to cheat them out of the maximum value to be gained from the trip.

It was hot on the Acropolis, but hotter still down in Constitution Square, where the sheep were allowed to disperse for a few minutes before getting back into their coach and being driven to the ship. Ludlow thankfully drank cold beer in one of the many cafés and nodded warily at David Acton who came in just after him. Apart from a brief explanation that Elizabeth and Diana were looking at the shops, Acton did not seem disposed to talk. It was only when everyone was straggling back to the coach that Ludlow noticed two small episodes that were to be remembered later. Elizabeth and Diana returned from their expedition, breathless and a little late but apparently quite happy. Elizabeth displayed a cheap vase, one of the thousands of imitations of the ancient red-figure vases which are turned out every year for tourists. Diana had a small but obviously expensive brooch in the peasant style. It was a delightful piece of work and received admiring exclamations from most of the women who were standing in the shade of an hotel and delaying as long as possible their entry into the hot coach.

"I'm afraid the Customs will charge you something for that," one of them said.

"So what?" Diana smiled in a bored sort of way. "There's nothing easier than paying, is there?"

Ludlow saw the look of anger, strong enough perhaps to be real hatred, which David Acton gave his sister for those words. The other incident which was to be remembered came when they were all crossing the dockside at Piraeus, trying to avoid the solicitations of sellers of vases, costumed dolls, souvenir ashtrays and other tokens of culture. Theresa Acton was walking alone as usual when her mother fell back from the drooping crowd and waited for her. Ludlow had stopped for a few moments to contemplate the *Inquirer* and satisfy himself that she was big enough and in good condition to continue the voyage. As he caught up and passed the two of them, he heard Elizabeth say,

"You must do something about it. You might kill a lot of people."

Ludlow did not linger to hear Theresa's reply, but she did not seem particularly troubled by her mother's warning.

The ship sailed in the early afternoon for Rhodes. The passengers disposed themselves about the deck to recover from the exertions of the morning and watch the shores of Greece slide away into the distance. It seemed as if a blue sky and sunshine were the necessary order of nature, destined to go on for ever and never to yield again to rain and fog. Ludlow sat and meditated happily on wet days when the whole college seemed to drip inside as well as out. Late in the afternoon, however, it became cooler and a wind started to come from what appeared to be the north, assuming that the ship was going the right way. Being a man of strong imagination, Ludlow travels prepared for disaster at any moment, and he now looked severely at the greyer sea which was slapping little waves against the side. He decided to go to his cabin and get a book to take his mind off the possibilities of disaster.

The main stairway from the promenade deck led to a large vestibule where the Cruise Office, like a hotel reception-desk, gave out landing-cards, changed travellers' cheques and generally nursed the ship's passengers in their various needs and anxieties. Cyril Burrows, the Cruise Director, was standing behind the desk, temporarily unoccupied but prepared to flash his toothy smile at anyone who might come and want something. He flashed one as Ludlow passed, a half-size one in consideration of the fact that this particular passenger did not occupy one of the most expensive cabins. Turning to descend the stairs to the next deck, Ludlow nearly collided with a fat and genial-looking man, wearing white flannels and a blazer with a badge of improbable heraldic significance. He looked as if he ought also to have a peaked yachting-cap, to show everybody that he was a real sailor.

"Sorry, old boy," this person said as Ludlow retreated and they both stood for a moment in the vestibule. "Just going below?"

"I am in fact going to my cabin," Ludlow said, reflecting that he had shown no sign of being about to climb the mast.

"Feel like lying down, what? Best thing if the old stomach's a bit upset."

"My stomach is quite well, thank you," Ludlow said with dignity.

"Good show. Let's hope it stays that way. It may get a bit choppy tonight. They often get these breezes among the islands, you know. They call this part the Sick Laids. Not bad, what?"

Ludlow went below without more words, unable to decide whether the man was a low comedian on holiday or was simply unable to pronounce Cyclades. He did not feel any happier for the prophecy of rough weather. However, the ship continued to move onwards with no more than a slight roll.

Consequently Ludlow was in the dining-saloon punctually and with a good appetite as usual. Being an early arrival by habit, he was always the first to sit down at the table for four to which he had been ushered on the first evening of the cruise. He read the menu and hoped that it would not be interfered with by any unpleasant change in the weather. Soon he was joined by the grey-haired American and his purple-haired wife, who were the friendliest of people but distressingly drank iced water with every course. The man had introduced himself on their first meeting as "Joseph P. Grossheim—in men's wear," which proved to refer to his job and not to his own attire. Both he and his wife, Cornelia, seemed to be enjoying every minute of their holiday and to be absorbing information at an alarming rate. Their frequent observations about the lack of air-conditioning in this part of the world were seemingly made more in sorrow than in anger.

This evening, as usual, Rupert Penge was the last to arrive at their table. As usual too, he apologized with an exaggerated bow and an amused glance at Ludlow's look of disapproval. Such looks tend to come involuntarily after years of dealing with unpunctual students. Ludlow could find no reason for disliking this young man, except a habitual distrust of excessive smartness and suavity in other males. Rupert Penge described himself as a barrister. He appeared to be unmarried and to be casting a hopeful eye at the more attractive women on the cruise. He was very quick on the draw with a silver and never-failing cigarette-lighter.

Dinner passed uneventfully, with polite talk about the wonders of Athens and the expected beauty of Rhodes. Ludlow was soon occupied with some excellent lobster and forgot all about the weather. He did have time, however, to glance at the Actons, whose table was near. The four of them sat together with the same air of constraint that had been noticeable on shore. It was also clear that Rupert Penge was impressed by Diana Acton and was determined to know her better.

After dinner, Ludlow found a sheltered corner in which to smoke his pipe and be thoughtful. He noted, without displeasure but with a slight and irrational disquiet, that Julie West had fallen in with the fat comedian in a blazer whom he had encountered earlier in the day. He wondered idly what kind of misinformation she would gather for her notebook. Yet there was something about the man, open and genial as he seemed to be, which was distinctly repellent. However, the cause of Anglo-American friendship was no doubt being served, and Ludlow was soon called upon to do his part by the arrival of Joseph P. Grossheim who came and sat down heavily beside him.

"It's a wonderful night. Cigarette? Oh, I see you've got a pipe. It's sure worth travelling all this way to see it."

"There doesn't appear to be anything much to see at the moment."

"Well, I mean the whole thing. That old Parthenon was just about the most wonderful thing I've ever seen. I reckon we've still got something to learn from those old-time people."

"Indeed we have," Ludlow said, cheering up at the chance of starting one of his general condemnations of the state of things. "To begin with, we might well re-establish respect for the drama as a meaningful and indeed religious expression of the society in which it appears. A little more thought for the classical studies which most of our Cabinet Ministers endured without comprehending them while they were at Eton. . . ."

"Yeah. Sure. I guess you've thought a lot about these things. You're a professor, aren't you?"

"I am a university teacher. Our grades are somewhat different from yours. In America I think I should rank as an Assistant Professor."

"It's a swell job to be doing. Have you ever been to our country, Professor?"

"No, perhaps I will one day."

Ludlow was spared from the need for any more near-perjury, because Grossheim's attention now switched to Diana Acton, who walked past like a model at a fashion parade, even managing to keep her hair unruffled in the wind.

"Do you know that lady?" Grossheim asked abruptly.

"I haven't spoken to her. I believe she's travelling with her brother and sister-in-law and their daughter."

"She is very fine-looking, don't you think?"

"She's very attractive, certainly. Almost uncomfortably so, one would have thought."

"Now you have a point there, Professor. I wouldn't want to say anything against Miss Diana Acton. No, sir, I wouldn't want to do anything of the kind. But I will say that I consider that she means trouble."

"Really? In what way?"

"I just wouldn't know. I consider that she means a whole load of trouble, for herself and for other people too. If you'll pardon my advice, I think you ought to stay right away from that woman. I wouldn't want to see a nice guy like you mixed up with her."

"I haven't the least intention of getting mixed up with her," Ludlow said. "I haven't come to my age to become involved with a woman who, apart from anything else, obviously has most expensive tastes."

"Expensive. Yeah, you've made a point there."

Whatever point Ludlow had made, it was not to be developed. An unmistakable voice was borne to them on the wind, uttering with a rising inflection the name "Joseph."

"I guess that's my wife," Grossheim said, getting quickly to his feet. "Pardon me, Professor. And, by the way, I'd appreciate it if you didn't say anything about our little talk. Coming, honey."

He trotted off, leaving Ludlow to smoke his pipe and look at the stars. The feeling of unease which had been growing during the day was stronger. He felt sure that this was not going to be an entirely happy cruise for some people, and that the Actons were going to be the most deeply involved. Eventually he went to his cabin, where he was not much cheered by the picture which the company had thoughtfully hung on the wall. It was a reproduction of a nineteenth-century engraving, and was called "The Wreck of the Steamship *San Francisco*."

— 2 —

The possibilities of evil seemed to have disappeared by the following morning. Ludlow awoke to find the ship at rest, anchored a few hundred yards outside the little harbour of Rhodes. The island gleamed across that stretch of sea which was lucidly blue without a trace of grey or green, drawing him out of bed with an enthusiasm which the colder mornings of London never managed to produce. Marvelling at his own athleticism, he even walked once round the deck before breakfast.

In a world that has made queues a necessity, the British are storing up great reserves of merit for themselves in the matter of patience. While a pair of motor-launches buzzed between the ship and the shore, a line of passengers stretched through the vestibule amidships and up the stairway to the promenade deck. Clutching cameras, landing-cards and straw hats, they waited with a simple faith that all things would be as they had been promised. Ludlow, always in good time for anything that interests him, was well to the front and getting ready to descend the steps which had been swung down the ship's side when he was pushed back by an enormous woman in a bright orange dress. Excusing herself in the politest French, she ploughed her way to the opening and disappeared with a speed that belied her fatness and suggested that she had special information that the ship was about to blow up. Ludlow was left feeling very British and noble, to make his own descent at a calmer rate.

The small launch was allowed to fill with what seemed

to be an alarming amount of people before it cast off, circled away from the comforting protection of the ship and headed towards the shore. However, it did not sink under the burden and they were very soon gliding past the column surmounted with the image of a stag which marked the entrance to the harbour. Burrows and his assistant were waiting on the quay, gentle as lambs but insistent as sheep-dogs, to see that they all got safely into the coaches which were waiting to take them to Lindos. They drove through the hills, ever rising towards their destination, past white villages of tiny houses and fields that were bleached after the long months of drought.

In spite of the steady climb, the acropolis of Lindos still rose high above them when they arrived. Donkeys waited to carry them to the summit. Ludlow looked thoughtfully at several of these creatures, observed latent wickedness in their eyes, calculated the discomfort they would cause to his long legs and bony frame, and decided to walk. While the donkeys clattered off up the rock-strewn side of the mountain, he joined the energetic and the timid who took the path through the village and past the little Byzantine church. Among these were the Grossheims, Cornelia wearing bright and tight pink trousers and complaining of the heat.

"I guess I can't climb another step in these pants," she was announcing as Ludlow overtook them.

"Cornelia's pants are strictly for standing up and looking beautiful in," Joseph Grossheim explained to Ludlow.

Being unable honestly to express agreement with the second part of this statement, Ludlow smiled benevolently and went on climbing. Grossheim was still looking worried, watching Cornelia with attention that seemed to have more of anxiety than affectionate concern. He also looked over his shoulder frequently, as if afraid of pursuit.

Ludlow began to wish that he had taken a donkey after all, as the sun grew hotter and the way steeper and his clothes proved still more unsuitable for his present purpose. He was so glad to reach the top that he did not even flinch away from the immediate approach of Julie West.

"If bears were bees, they'd build their nests at the bottom of trees," he said pleasantly.

"Pardon me, Professor?"

"Nothing. Did you come up on a donkey?"

"I sure did, but nothing will induce me to go down on it. I was just terrified, the way that crazy animal sort of went sideways all the time as if it was trying to make me fall off. I don't know why they don't have a lift coming up here. Surely they could make a hole right through these old rocks."

"I've no doubt that the wonders of science would tear a hole through Lindos with the greatest of pleasure, and then use the stones of the acropolis for cement. Never mind, it won't be so bad walking down. Now let's look at the view."

It was indeed worth looking at. Far beneath them the sea lay like a still lake, with only the thinnest line of white where it came gently to rest on the sand. The village of Lindos was a child's model, perfect in every detail. They stood and looked down on an island which had felt the impact of many civilizations, in their glory and their greed. Crusaders now were at peace with the Greeks whose walls they had taken and built up again.

While Julie was seeing the world as usual through the view-finder of her camera, Ludlow slipped away to explore the place on his own. Like all middle-aged bachelors whose friends are married and therefore not available for distant holidays, he has learned to enjoy his own company and to observe his companions with interest but without regret. The reality of the present gradually broke through his musing on the past. He saw Diana Acton, cool and unruffled as ever, a figure to catch the attention even at this place where there was heavy competition from more static beauty. She was with the fat humorist who had spoken to Ludlow on the previous day and had been talking to Julie West in the evening. He certainly seemed to be able to get on with an assortment of different types, for

Diana was now listening with attention to what he was saying. Ludlow decided that he was giving her a great deal of cheerful misinformation about Rhodes and its history; since she would have forgotten it all by the end of the cruise, it mattered little whether she was told the truth or not. But why did she stand so stiffly, and clench her hands, and turn away to look out over the sea? Ludlow wished that he could watch her face and hear what the fat man was saying to her.

Rupert Penge approached them, his face pre-set in the facetious smile which he obviously imagined to be one of his principal charms. He spoke to Diana, trying to ignore her companion, who had no intention of being ignored. Curiosity struggled with politeness, as Ludlow watched the three of them together. It seemed that both the men were producing the same brand of humour, annoying each other with it and boring Diana. Eventually, just as curiosity was winning and making Ludlow start to come nearer to them, Diana said something to Rupert which made him go red, shut his mouth quickly and turn away. The fat man took her by the arm and led her to a more distant corner of the site. It seemed an unlikely victory, but Lindos no doubt had witnessed stranger scenes than this. Rupert strode past Ludlow, his face set and angry. A few moments later, a quiet voice said, "Beast." Ludlow turned, to see Theresa Acton standing a few paces behind him; she too had obviously been watching what had happened.

"I beg your pardon, Miss Acton," Ludlow said politely, wondering whether she meant him.

Theresa started, appeared to blush under her make-up and suddenly looked very young and unprotected. Ludlow looked at her with compassion; years of work with students had taught him to recognize the frailty and tension beneath the affectations that the young use to cover their insecurity.

"Sorry," Theresa said. "I hadn't noticed that you were here. I was looking at her."

"Your aunt, you mean?"

"I like to hear you calling her that." Theresa giggled.

"She is your aunt, isn't she? I spend a good deal of my professional life trying to persuade people to call things by their right names, so I see no reason why I should——"

"Yes, of course she is, but she hates to be reminded of it—it makes her feel old, and she's terrified of that. She's years younger than my father, you see, and she doesn't like having a grown-up niece. I call her Aunt Diana when I want to annoy her."

"Does that happen very often?" Ludlow asked.

"All the time. I hate her."

"Really? She seems to be a very attractive woman."

"Oh, you would think that. All the men fall for her, and she encourages it. I hate men too," she added tersely.

"I'm sorry to hear it."

"Not you. I mean silly young men."

Ludlow decided to take comfort from "silly" and ignore "young". They walked together towards the steps, where Burrows was being a sheep-dog again and the donkeys waited.

"Let's walk down," Theresa suggested.

"By all means," said Ludlow, feeling rather pleased with the situation. "I feel even less inclined to entrust myself to one of those creatures than I did on the way up. Your—er—aunt appears to be in good hands."

"I can't imagine why she's decided to get her claws into Adrian Mallaby," she said. Ludlow noted the name.

"Perhaps she likes him," he said.

"She can't possibly. He hangs about and makes silly remarks all the time. And he must be even older than you. She just likes to show off."

"It's rather surprising that she's never got married," said Ludlow, probing.

"She'd rather play around. She never lets them go all the way. The only thing that stops her is that she's so scared of losing her figure if she got pregnant. But perhaps she won't always have it all her own way."

"Why do you say that?" Ludlow asked, pitying her for trying to shock him and also growing interested in the conversation.

"I don't know—she can't go on having all the luck. Life isn't like that. I don't believe that anybody can be happy for ever. Something's bound to happen to her."

"I ought not to form an opinion after a few days' observation. It is extremely unwise to jump to conclusions, and the academic mind must consider a great deal of evidence before deciding anything. I suppose this is what is known as the scientific method, a curious irony by which scientists have now arrogantly taken to themselves the foundations of knowledge——"

"What are you trying to say?" Theresa asked. Ludlow, unused to interruptions from young people, looked severely at her before replying.

"I was about to remark," he said, "that I very much doubt whether she can be described as a happy woman."

"Well, she damn well ought to be, with her looks and her money."

"Oh, she has money, has she?"

"I thought that would interest you. That's what always draws them most. But you needn't think you'll get hold of it, because she's horribly mean."

"I've no intention of trying," Ludlow said, with a last effort to be patient with this suffering but difficult girl.

They were coming back into the village now, reaching the last part of their descent. The donkey-riders were already down, busily buying postcards to assure their friends and themselves that they had really been here. Others swallowed dark, cool liquids at a stall close to where the coaches waited. Theresa looked up at him, her eyes seeming to plead beneath their artificial shadows.

"She's got all the family money," she said, repeating the words like a recitation painfully learned. "We scarcely have enough to live on. I know that they had to borrow from her to come on this trip, though they didn't tell me about it. But she did. She always does something to spoil things for me. I hate her, and I wish she was dead."

There was chill in the sun that was now reaching its zenith. Diana and the man who was called Adrian Mallaby were not far behind them, and Ludlow wondered whether he could speak a warning without being classed as a silly old man instead of a silly young one. Before he could do so, Theresa spoke.

"Don't you start to hate me too," she said.

Then she ran away towards Rupert Penge, who was sulking in the shade of one of the coaches, and began trying to match his humour and his attempt at worldly cynicism. Ludlow did not take very much notice of the scenery on the long drive back to the harbour.

They visited the town of Rhodes in the afternoon, and sailed at teatime, which is observed as religiously on British ships as on more static parts of British territory. The island sank out of sight as if the placid sea had indeed swallowed it and left only a nostalgic smear on the horizon. The *Inquirer* turned her bows towards the setting sun, beginning the two days' sailing to Malta. The passengers relaxed in the prospect of uninterrupted sunbathing, their memory of Rhodes already becoming confused with their memory of Athens. Since people who have set out to enjoy themselves must always be made to do so, Burrows tinnily announced over the ship's loudspeakers that there would be games and novelty dances in the main lounge that evening. Ludlow shuddered, and resolved to read in his cabin.

It was not to be. After dinner, Joseph Grossheim took his arm affectionately and said that they were all going to have a lot of fun that evening. Ludlow is a polite and kindly man, in spite of his frequent outbursts against certain sections of the human race, and he allowed himself to be guided to the main lounge and seated at a table which commanded a good view. The centre of the floor had been cleared for dancing, and the ship's band was already making experimental noises. The prospect of boredom was completed when Julie West appeared and was invited to join them. The band started to play and a few couples drifted on to the floor. Ludlow sat firmly in his chair, while Grossheim danced energetically with Cornelia and then with Julie. Fortified by whisky, he was able to talk each time to the solitary woman in spite of the competition provided by music in a small room.

Cyril Burrows, oozing good-fellowship and impeccable in a white uniform, announced that the next dance would be a Prize Elimination Dance. Grossheim took Cornelia into the fray. Nearly all the tables were gradually abandoned.

"Everyone on the floor, please," Burrows exhorted.

"Wouldn't you love to try this, Professor?" Julie asked plaintively.

"I can't dance," Ludlow said firmly.

"Oh, come on. It doesn't matter."

The floor was by now so crowded that it did indeed seem that it would not matter. Ludlow grunted resentfully and allowed himself to be led out. He shuffled around, hoping to be eliminated as soon as possible. The floor gradually emptied, as Burrows expelled men who were wearing pink socks and women who had not sent a postcard from Rhodes. The Grossheims disappeared in a grand exodus of husbands and wives dancing together, after which they sat and shouted encouragement to Ludlow and Julie. Ludlow thought miserably of getting out by cheating, as the amount of space increased and his own deficiencies became more apparent. After he had kicked Julie involuntarily for the sixth time, and was feeling ready to do it deliberately, he was sent off as one of the men wearing a striped shirt. He returned thankfully to his table, calling for cold beer.

As the evening progressed, he acquired a paper hat, which he reluctantly put on, and a false moustache which he ignored. A number of paper streamers attached themselves to him. If it's like this now, he thought, what on earth will they get up to at the end of the voyage? The dancing became more feverish and the music more incomprehensible. However, he decided that he was enjoying himself. It was, he thought, at least a change from routine. Diana Acton danced past with Adrian Mallaby. The fat man danced lightly and with ease, talking to Diana about something which appeared to be holding her interest. Ludlow sadly decided, not for the first time in his life, that there were some men who could and some men who couldn't.

"Isn't it lovely to see Diana enjoying herself?" Julie said, with what might have been a reproachful look at Ludlow.

"Yes, indeed," said Ludlow, sitting firmly where he was.

"Sometimes I think that she hasn't ever gotten much real happiness out of life."

"Do you know her well?" Ludlow showed some interest in this last remark.

"Oh no, but you know I've been sharing a cabin with her since the second day out—after she had that dreadful quarrel with Theresa."

"Have you? What makes you think she isn't happy?"

"I guess it isn't anything particularly. It's just the sort of thing you feel when you talk to a person for a while. She's a swell girl, though. Don't you think so, Mr. Grossheim?"

"Yeah, sure." Joseph Grossheim looked as though he wished he were somewhere else. Cornelia looked at the ceiling. Invisible icicles formed.

"Oh, have I said something I shouldn't? Isn't that just like me! My old schoolteacher used to say to me, 'Julie, that silly tongue of yours will get you into trouble one of these days.' Have I said anything wrong, Professor?"

"Not as far as I'm aware," Ludlow said. "I think it's time we had something to drink."

The moment passed. Ludlow sat back, looking abstracted and innocent, and prepared to absorb any further bits of information. He felt more than ever that some kind of trouble was building up. As he appeared to look vaguely at the dancers, he was watching Cyril Burrows. The Cruise Director had relinquished the microphone for a time and was standing by the side of the bar. His professional smile was fixed as usual; but there was an instant when it was replaced by a scowl when Adrian and Diana danced past him. Ludlow wondered for which of them it was intended. Then Burrows passed in less than a second from a scowl, through a smile, to a look of alarm. Theresa was at his side, smiling at him, apparently asking him something. Burrows looked like a trapped man, in mortal danger. But Theresa seemed to be satisfied by his answer, and went back to the table where she had been sitting with her parents.

What about David and Elizabeth Acton? Ludlow's eyes followed Theresa back to their table. They seemed happy enough, watching Theresa with that look of mingled apprehension and relief which parents give to a difficult daughter who is behaving well unexpectedly. He thought that he saw hostility on their faces too, when Diana and Adrian passed them, but decided that he was getting too imaginative. Then Rupert went and asked Theresa to dance, which she did, trying to mask her obvious pleasure with an unbecoming frown. Rupert danced well, as might have been supposed. But since the floor was now more crowded than ever, it was not surprising that he soon pushed against Adrian and Diana. It was happening all the time: indeed, the floor appeared to be the scene of conflict rather than recreation. But Adrian stopped, to the interruption of the shuffling stream, and said, "That was bloody clumsy."

Ludlow watched, with detached but strong interest, this revelation of another side to the facetious comedian. Adrian was red, and Rupert was white. Diana and Theresa both stood and looked at each other. It was as if the quarrel were really between them, the men merely being puppets that they controlled to do their fighting for them. The band valiantly played on, but the dancers slowed to the slightest pretence of movement.

"You got in my way," Rupert said. "You're always getting in my way."

"What exactly do you mean by that?"

It's Neolithic Man, Ludlow thought. Two are fighting over one, while the rest of us watch and hope to see something exciting. He felt sorry for Theresa, though her pale mask showed no emotion. Then Burrows was at the microphone again.

"Thank you very much, ladies and gentlemen. Clear the floor, please. The next dance will be a Novelty Spot Dance, with prizes for the lucky couples."

Civilization asserted itself under the thin veneer of a white uniform and a pink, well-shaven face. Rupert and Adrian glared at each other and turned away. This was no longer the age when men fought and killed for their women. Or was it? Ludlow was not at all sure.

Though Burrows sweatingly exhorted them, the dancers never regained their enthusiasm. Gradually the lounge emptied. Julie and the Grossheims, all more subdued than usual, went off to their cabins. Ludlow was thankfully set free to lean over the stern rail, smoking his pipe and watching the white wake of the ship. Above, it was a perfect and calm night. Below, what storms were gathering? Two remarks ran through his head and tried to make their own illogical pattern. Theresa at Lindos, saying fiercely, "Something's bound to happen to her." And Julie, quoting in her embarrassment, "That silly tongue of yours will get you into trouble one of these days." Perhaps it was not only the contrast with the heat of the lounge which made the night seem rather cold.

— 3 —

It was a strange thing, Ludlow reflected, how quickly time passes at sea. If this were London, a free afternoon would present many challenges from books unread, exhibitions unvisited and essays uncorrected. Yet this blue conspiracy of sea and sky, which ought to cause boredom and frustration in a man who takes a Johnsonian view of life outside the metropolis, soothed the hours between meals without allowing the unsuspecting traveller to fret about time wasted. He settled himself contentedly in a long deck-chair near the stern, taking a corner where he could observe his fellow-passengers and at the same time keep an eye on the sea to make sure that it did not misbehave itself. Stretching out his tweed-clad legs, he cautiously rolled up his sleeves and exposed his arms to the sun. He made a little pile of his necessary equipment for the afternoon: book, tin of cream which offered "a golden tan without burning," pipe, tobacco pouch, matches, sunglasses—where on earth were the sunglasses? A circular sweep of his long arm brought them from under the chair to join the rest on his lap. There really did seem to be a lot of things to do before one could settle down, and he sighed momentarily for the comfortable chaos of his far-distant desk, where at least he could be sure of finding things.

Ludlow opened his book, but directed his attention for a time to the rail of the deck. He watched the gentle roll of the horizon between its bars, until he had satisfied himself that the ship was in no immediate danger of turning completely over.

Now it was time to settle down to his book. But his

attention was distracted again, by the sight of Rupert and Theresa together by the tiny swimming-pool. In spite of her strictures against young men, Theresa seemed contented enough. In a bathing-costume, and without the fantastic make-up that she usually had, she looked much prettier and also very young and vulnerable. Rupert was obviously well pleased with himself and Theresa even permitted herself to laugh at one of his attempts to be amusing. They both seemed more attractive in each other's company than they did individually. Meditating on this fact, Ludlow sank into a pleasant doze.

He returned to wakefulness at the sound of a chair being scraped across the deck towards his own. Elizabeth Acton was negotiating herself into a place where he could hardly ignore her. He grunted politely and remarked on the weather, as Englishmen do in all parts of the world. Elizabeth moved her chair a little nearer and asked him if he knew the name of an island that was faintly visible to the north. Ludlow said that he had no idea.

"That reminds me," Elizabeth said brightly, "I was wanting to ask you something. There's a poem that says something about the isles of Greece. I can't remember it exactly, but I read it at school. I'm sure it's by Tennyson, but Theresa says it's by Shelley."

"Really? And what does your husband say?"

"Oh, David isn't interested in poetry. I thought you might be able to tell me who wrote it."

"As a matter of fact, it was Byron."

Ludlow quoted at some length, as he does on the least provocation. Elizabeth listened in respectful silence until he had finished.

"Byron, is it? Well, I was sure it was Tennyson. It sounded like him, somehow. Things aren't always what they seem."

"Many things are not what they seem, Mrs. Acton—and many people too."

Ludlow wondered what she really wanted with him; he soon found out.

"Did you get on well with Theresa, Mr. Ludlow? I saw you having a little talk with her yesterday, on the way down that awful hill. I thought how nice it was for her to show an interest in an older man."

"She was kind enough to accompany me on my feeble and senile descent from Lindos. She seems a very agreeable young person."

"I'm so glad you thought so, because people do tend to get the wrong impression about her. I mean, that awful make-up she wears and the rude things she says to everybody. She really is very difficult sometimes. David says it's just a phase."

"I'm sure he's right. The young always take up some extreme attitude, if they have any character at all. In two or three years, you'll find her indignantly denying that she was ever like this. How old is she?"

"Seventeen. But sometimes she acts like a child, and then next minute she frightens me by seeming so mature. She says the most awful things—I can't think where she learns them. I do hope she doesn't get herself into any sort of trouble."

"I think she's a sensible girl, basically. She's at an age for threatening death and destruction to everyone who annoys her, but it doesn't mean anything."

Elizabeth started, and seemed to shiver in the sunlight. Theresa and Rupert had walked away from the pool and were leaning over the rail on the other side of the ship.

"Why did you say that, Mr. Ludlow—about death and destruction?" Her voice was sharp, perhaps with anger or with fear.

"I've seen a long succession of students who believe that they can accomplish anything by being indignant about it. Learning to live with injustice is one of the lessons of growing up."

"Did Theresa say anything to you about death, or killing?"

"Certainly not. It was just a manner of speaking."

"I'm sorry." Elizabeth relaxed. "I get so anxious about

Theresa sometimes. And things have been going wrong, ever since we started on this cruise. I wish we hadn't come, but David thought it would do us good. Did Theresa tell you about the cabin?"

"She told me nothing."

"Well, you see, the original idea was for Diana and Theresa to share a cabin next door to David's and mine. I ought to have known it wouldn't work out. They quarrelled dreadfully the first night, and Diana said she'd fly back from Athens and leave us. And that would have spoiled everything."

It would indeed, Ludlow thought, since she was helping to finance the holiday for you.

"What did they quarrel about?" he asked in a tone of idle curiosity.

"Oh, just silly things. About who was going to have which bed, and about Diana taking up too much room in the wardrobe. No real reason, but I might have known something like that would happen."

"Your daughter doesn't like her aunt?"

"It's difficult for all of us. It's not Diana's fault, but then you can't blame Theresa for thinking that it is."

Ludlow sat up and banished his drowsiness in a desire to learn more. His sense of trouble lurking in this family was evidently justified.

"What isn't her fault?" he asked.

"About the money. I'm afraid that's what's spoilt her—I mean, made her rather inconsiderate of others. You see, when David's father died, Diana was only about the same age as Theresa is now. There was a big gap in age between her and David, and she was always the favourite. Old Mr. Acton was afraid that she wouldn't be able to look after herself and he wanted to make sure that she would always be well provided for." Elizabeth sniffed meaningly.

"So he left her all his money?" Ludlow prompted her.

"Yes, nearly all of it. He left the business to David, but without enough money to carry it on properly. It's only a small firm, and it can't really stand up to the competition of the bigger ones. And I'm afraid that David isn't as good a business-man as his father was. So life really has been rather difficult."

"Doesn't Miss Acton help financially?"

"She lends David money sometimes, but she always insists on having it back as soon as he can pay it. I don't know why she should behave like that to her own brother. She seems terribly afraid of letting any money out of her possession—except to buy clothes or jewels for herself. Anyone would think she was in danger of becoming poor."

"That is often an obsessive fear of the rich. The miser, who appears so often in our literature, is by no means a product solely of the imagination. And although we think of the personal parsimony of a Scrooge or a Silas Marner, there are other instances where avarice is combined with self-indulgence to a remarkable degree—but what happened about the cabin?"

Elizabeth, unaccustomed to Ludlow's switches of interest in the middle of a sentence, looked at him without comprehension.

"It is clear to observation that Miss Acton did not in fact fly home from Athens," he explained patiently. "I assume therefore that some quite satisfactory arrangement was made."

"Oh, yes. It was difficult, because apparently there aren't many single cabins on the ship, and there wasn't one vacant. Diana had quite a row with Mr. Burrows about it, but there wasn't anything the poor man could do. Then Miss West happened to overhear them talking, and she offered to change with Theresa. So Theresa went into her place in a cabin with a French lady, and Miss West came in with Diana. It was very good of her, wasn't it?"

"Most kind. I suppose her self-sacrifice may be measured to some extent by the character of the French lady whose company she was leaving."

"Well, Theresa says that she does snore terribly. Still,

it saved the situation for us, because Diana seems to get on well with the American girl—and we're all still close together because Theresa's new cabin is right opposite ours."

"I'm glad to hear such a happy ending to the story." Ludlow was beginning to lose interest, and wondered as he often did why people came and confided their affairs to him so readily. Admittedly, it had proved useful once or twice in the past, when there was a mystery to be solved. But there was no possibility of violent death on this holiday ship . . . was there?

"Your daughter seems to have found solace this afternoon," he said.

Elizabeth looked across at Theresa and Rupert.

"Yes, she does," she said slowly. "Mr. Ludlow, what do you know about that young man?"

"Very little. He sits at my table for meals, and I gather that he describes himself as a barrister. He has a brand of humour which does not particularly appeal to me."

"He tried to get friendly with Diana during the first couple of days," Elizabeth said, "but she soon brushed him off. She likes to have men going after her, but she never encourages them for long. She thinks they're all after her money, and I dare say she's right."

"Money apart, she's a very attractive young woman."

"I suppose she is." Elizabeth got up abruptly. "Thank you for listening to me. You won't repeat any of this, will you?"

"I am well used to keeping confidences, Mrs. Acton."

So Diana was at odds with her family, Ludlow thought after Elizabeth had gone. She had also had some degree of unpleasantness with Rupert Penge, and with Cyril Burrows, the Cruise Director. Yet she seemed to be on friendly terms with the improbable Adrian Mallaby. It was all very interesting. He dozed again, remembering his promise not to repeat what he had heard; it was a promise that was not to be kept.

The sun moved slowly down the sky, the light breeze turned high summer into friendly autumn. The *Inquirer* moved on steadily through the water, passing among islands that had watched the passing of ships long before Byron came to sing of them. Gradually the passengers began to drift away to their cabins. Towels and wraps were damply gathered from beside the pool. It was time to get ready for dinner. Ludlow stirred himself, got up and dropped his little collection on the deck, picked up the bits and walked away with a cheerful nautical roll.

Diana was sitting with Julie West at one of the small tables that were dotted about the sun-deck. She stretched lazily, magnificent in a bathing-costume which had cost more than some of the dresses that were worn in the lounge.

"Time to go and change for dinner," she said.

"I guess it is." Julie got up.

"Really, I could stay here all night," Diana said. "I don't think I want dinner. They serve such enormous meals on this ship."

"You ought to get something to eat," Julie said.

"Perhaps I'll have a tray in the cabin. Let's go and have a glass of sherry, anyway. I've got a bottle."

"That would be just fine."

They went down the stairway to the promenade deck. Adrian Mallaby stood aside to let them pass. The smile which he gave Diana was very pleasant; but his smile when she had passed him was a different kind of smile altogether.

The dining-saloon was ready for the hungry passengers to come to dinner. Each table was white with its cloth and folded napkins, shining with cutlery all laid in the right place. The flowers in their vases stirred very slightly in the breeze which was drifting through the half-opened windows. It was a pleasant room, rising out of the promenade deck and with a high ceiling which could roll back to open under the night sky. There was a sense almost of reverence, as if in preparation for some ritual that was continually repeated yet never lost its deep significance. The plain fact was that the passengers had paid large amounts of money to be there, and expected to be well served and fed.

In the adjacent pantry, a sweating fury belied the cool promise of the saloon. Was it possible that suave attention would be given in a few minutes by this mass of men who cursed and jostled each other as they pulled on white coats? The smell of soup floated around them, tantalizing them with promise of food that was not for them. The telephone on the Chief Steward's desk rang. He picked it up, already shaping his lips to give the appropriate response to an officer, a passenger, or an underling.

"Very good, madam. I'll have a tray prepared at once, and your cabin stewardess will bring it down to you. Not at all, madam, it's not the least trouble."

He replaced the telephone and looked round the crowded pantry. A short, dark-browed steward fell under his eye.

"Harmer," said the Chief Steward, "there's a job for you. One of your passengers wants a tray in her cabin instead of coming to dinner. Just fruit and orange juice, she says. Get cracking on it."

"Blimey," Harmer said with an air of outrage, "couldn't she make up her mind before this? How the hell am I going to get a tray ready and be out in time to serve the first course? Who is it?"

"It's a particular friend of yours, as it happens. Miss Acton."

Harmer gave his opinion of Miss Acton profanely and at some length. The Chief Steward picked up the telephone again. A few minutes later, Diana's stewardess came in answer to his call. A tray, discreetly covered with a cloth, had been prepared by the indignant Harmer.

"Mind you don't drop it," said the Chief Steward, pinching her as she went past.

The stewardess replied in unladylike language, and went out with the tray. The pantry rose to its crisis of preparation. There were only five minutes left before dinner, and the Purser had a positive mania for punctual service.

Cyril Burrows had on his full-size smile for Cornelia Grossheim, who was changing American Express cheques and declaring that she just didn't know where she was with all these different currencies. Burrows was more than willing to explain them to her, though his short lecture on international finance merely evoked surprise that everyone could not agree to use dollars. Adrian Mallaby, waiting to change the less-honoured English pound, smiled and ventured a few bright remarks which were not well taken. While Cornelia was signing her cheques, the stewardess came down the main stairway and started to cross the foyer.

"Where are you taking that tray?" Burrows asked her.

"To a passenger's cabin," the stewardess said shortly. It was no business of the Cruise Director to ask questions. His job was to look after the passengers and their shore-excursions. Anything else he had to say ought to come through the Purser. She knew her place, and she liked——

"I didn't think you were taking it to the engine-room," said Burrows, breaking into her reverie. "Who is it for?"

"Miss Diana Acton," said the stewardess. There was no sense in looking for trouble.

"Let me see it. Miss Acton is very particular."

The tray was put down on the side of the counter. Burrows took it to the back of his little office, and examined it critically.

"It seems all right," he said. "Is Miss Acton unwell?"

"I don't think so. She's asked for a tray before when she didn't want much to eat."

"All right, take it down. And be sure you give it to her properly, into her own hands."

"She said I was to leave it outside the door," the stewardess replied, turning briskly into the corridor which led to the forward cabins.

"Now, Mrs. Grossheim," Burrows said with a large smile, "you want to change fifty dollars...."

— 4 —

The ice in Ludlow's dry Martini slowly dissolved. The evening was still warm, though the sky had softened to violet and there was enough breeze to throw up a light foam against the bows. To sit on deck at this moment, glowing with a day's absorption of sun, was to reach a rare degree of joy. Dinner would be served in ten minutes; and until then he could be alone, without anyone forcing him into unnecessary conversation.

"Oh, Professor, isn't this just the most marvellous evening!"

Julie West dropped into the chair next to him. Ludlow sadly registered the thought that he had spent his life being persecuted by women who bored him and avoided by those who attracted him. He looked with distaste at the eager expression now turned upon him, before rebuking himself for his lack of charity.

"It is certainly very beautiful," he said, with a forced smile which startled Julie considerably.

"I guess those old Greeks would find it strange to see a big ship like this going along past their islands," she said.

"No stranger perhaps than we should find one of theirs. Relative size is not too difficult for the mind to grasp, compared with other changes. The Greeks would probably be more surprised by our devotion to technical change, which we are pleased to call progress. They had little faith in progress as a concept of history. It was the cyclical view which attracted them."

"Yeah. Well, isn't it interesting to think of that."

Julie was not the first to find Ludlow's light conversation rather heavy going. With an effort, he tried another level.

"I suppose Miss Acton will be up to join us soon," he said.

"Well, no, Diana's not coming to dinner."

"Dear me, I'm sorry to hear that. Is she ill?" asked Ludlow, who could think of no other reason for missing dinner.

"No, she's fine. But she thought she wouldn't bother with dinner because she wasn't feeling hungry. They do give us such colossal meals on this ship, that you have to miss one sometimes. It's not so bad when we've had a long day on shore, but after a day like this I just haven't any appetite. Still, I thought I'd come and eat a little. But it's hard to get enough exercise in that little swimming-pool."

"It certainly is," said Ludlow cheerfully, not having tried to get any exercise at all. "However, one ought to eat something."

"Diana's going to have some fruit sent down to her cabin, so I guess she'll be all right. I'll go down right after dinner and make sure she's eaten something."

"Very good. I understand that you avoided a crisis in the Acton family by being willing to change your cabin." Ludlow had grown more and more curious and decided that he might as well use this forced conversation to learn some more. The vague sense of anxiety which had been with him all day was still troubling him.

"Gee, that was nothing at all. I was glad to help."

"It was an act of kindness."

"It was more an act of selfishness, really." Julie giggled and looked alarmingly coy. "Say, Professor, can you keep a secret?"

"Most certainly I can," said Ludlow, not altogether truthfully.

"Well, I was just desperate to change my cabin after the first night. I was sharing with a French lady, and she really was too awful. She snored all night, and she wanted the whole place to herself. She had five suitcases, and there was scarcely any room for my things. And would you believe it, she could hardly understand English."

"Very remiss of her. So you too were ready for a change?"

"I sure was. I was standing by that place downstairs where they change the money, waiting to ask if they could find me another cabin. And Diana was there, going on at that nice man Mr. Burrows and saying that something had to be done. She was being a bit rude to him, I thought. Anyway, I took the chance and said I wouldn't mind changing."

"So all ended happily. That is, if Miss Acton is a more congenial companion than your temporary Gallic friend."

"Oh, Diana's swell. We get along like anything. I guess all the trouble with her family is that she has the money and they want it. Having all that money has made her a bit difficult. But at heart she's just a fine, homely sort of girl. I only hope it doesn't make me get a lot of enemies too."

"Hope that what doesn't?" asked Ludlow, finding Julie's train of thought difficult to follow.

"Having money. Shall I tell you another secret? I came into a lot of money, just three months ago. That's why I was able to take this wonderful trip to Europe. At home I'm just an ordinary schoolteacher, and I never thought I'd be able to get so far away for my vacation. But an uncle died who'd grown pretty rich in real estate. I'd scarcely heard of him, but it seems that I was his only close relative, and he left practically everything to me. So now I've given up my teaching job, and when I get back I'm going to start in and learn all about the business."

"My congratulations," said Ludlow when Julie at last paused for breath. "Are you going straight back at the end of this cruise?"

"I might stop over in Britain for a few days. I'd sure like to see the old country. My grandfather came from a place called Liverpool. And maybe we could meet up in London, and you could show me round Buckingham Palace."

Ludlow was saved by the gentle but penetrating sound of the gong which was beaten around the deck when dinner was served. They went into the dining-saloon, and separated towards their different tables. Ludlow greeted his steward and eagerly read the menu. Then he sat, and wondered why other people could not be punctual for meals. As usual, the gong seemed to be regarded as a first warning instead of as a signal to start eating. The stewards stood around with their arms folded and waited for the places to be filled. Julie had sat down opposite Adrian Mallaby, who must have been there even before the gong went. He was looking pleased with himself as usual, and engaged Julie in a flow of conversation which made her laugh a lot and blush a little. Soon they were joined by an elderly couple, taking their first holiday for years and enjoying it like children. Glaring hungrily over the menu, Ludlow saw David and Elizabeth Acton come in together and sit at the table next to his. They looked serious and unhappy and did not speak.

Eventually Joseph Grossheim puffed up to his chair next to Ludlow, explaining that Cornelia was not coming to dinner.

"She's kind of worried about her figure," he whispered like a conspirator. "I tell her she doesn't have to worry, she's got a swell figure and I ought to know. But she gets this idea that she ought not to eat too much. And I think maybe she's had a bit too much sun today. So she's just lying down quiet."

"I hope she will be all right. Isn't she having something sent down on a tray?"

"She won't touch a thing. I did see a tray though, being put outside the cabin at the end of the corridor, near to ours. Looks like someone else had the same idea."

"That will be for Miss Acton. I understand that she too has reached her present capacity and is not coming to dinner."

"That so?" Grossheim looked uncomfortable and fell silent.

The steward now decided that it was time to have pity on the waiting passengers, who had formed an adequate quorum for the ritual dinner. Ludlow took a lot of hors-d'oeuvres and sat happily chewing black olives and observing the room around him. Since Grossheim did not seem disposed to talk, Ludlow made no effort to encourage him.

Towards the end of the first course, Theresa Acton flounced her way to the table where her parents were already sitting. She was wearing a full pink dress which made her look very attractive but did not seem to modify her usual sullen expression. She waved away the offered dish and drank some water. Ludlow went on eating, and feeling sorry for women who worried about their figures.

Rupert Penge came soon after Theresa, to join Ludlow and Grossheim. He apologized in his facetious way and began to eat as if he had been starved for a week. Watching him, Ludlow thought that this was the voracity of worry rather than hunger. Penge was clearly not at ease. He carefully avoided looking at the Actons' table though he was in a position which made this effort awkward. Dinner moved on through its six courses, and an air of warm peace gradually suffused the saloon. Ludlow told himself that his premonitions were foolish. With the fierce self-depreciation which alternates with his moments of having a very good opinion of himself, he vowed not to start finding mysteries and dangers where none existed. What if Diana Acton seemed to have made a lot of enemies? That was no reason for imagining an aura of doom around her. He refilled his glass.

During the dessert, Adrian Mallaby went out. He

stopped and spoke to Ludlow, who had never said anything to him except during their brief encounter of the previous day.

"Can't take any more, old boy," Mallaby said. "Got to go out for a spot of fresh air on deck. They certainly look after the inner man on this ship."

He grinned at Ludlow, but as he turned away he darted a look of hatred at Rupert Penge. Ludlow wondered idly why a fat man like Mallaby could not finish his dinner, while he himself had a hearty appetite and remained thin. He took another peach.

Conversation at this table had not been bright during the meal. Both Grossheim and Penge seemed preoccupied and uncomfortable, and Ludlow was applying himself to his food as a full-time occupation. Now, however, they all relaxed and began to talk.

"Did you take any good pictures at Rhodes?" Grossheim asked.

"Neither good nor bad," said Ludlow, since the question seemed to be addressed to him.

"Why, don't you have a camera?" Grossheim looked as though Ludlow had confessed to losing his passport.

"I prefer a wider view than any instrument can give me. Besides, they always go wrong. The film seems to stick when I want to remove it. I haven't tried for a number of years now."

"You ought to get a new model, Mr. Ludlow. You wouldn't find it any trouble at all to manipulate. And it's good to have some pictures to remind you of places where you've been on vacation."

"I am content to depend on that inward eye which is the bliss of solitude, as Wordsworth put it."

"Yeah, sure. But I do like to have movies to show the folks back at home. Don't you have home-movie cameras in Britain?"

"No, the only cameras we can get need a tripod and a black cloth. It makes them unsuitable for use in hot countries."

"Well, that's too bad. I sure wouldn't like to be without my movie camera."

"Anyway," Rupert Penge said, "you can buy prepared transparencies for showing on a projector, at all the important places. It doesn't seem worth the trouble of taking your own, and not knowing until later whether they'll come out or not."

Grossheim shook his head at these signs of primitivism and decided to try a subject more suitable for Ancient Britons.

"Maybe you can tell me something," he said. "You remember yesterday in the afternoon, when we drove up above the town?"

"Yes, my memory goes back that far," said Ludlow.

"Well, didn't the guide show us some old ruins and say it was the Temple of Apollo? Now I'm pretty sure that the guide way back in Greece said the same thing. What was that place we drove out to, across that little canal?"

"Corinth."

"Sure. Now was there or was there not the Temple of Apollo there in Corinth? It looks like these guys are all trying to claim the same thing. I want to tell the folks that I've seen the genuine Temple of Apollo. Joseph P. Grossheim ain't going to be put off with no fakes. So which was the right one of those two?"

Ludlow became so busy explaining the common incidence of Temples of Apollo in the ancient world that he must have failed to notice David Acton going out. It was only at the end of his lecture that he realized Elizabeth and Theresa were alone at their table. Grossheim looked more confused than ever by the time Ludlow had finished, but he gave his opinion that it was a good trip and full of interesting things to see. The other two agreed.

"It makes it hell when you go back, though," Penge said unexpectedly. "I mean, one can live like this for two weeks in the year, and the rest of the time's just struggling to keep on. Two weeks of sunshine, and fifty weeks of London fog."

"There is comparatively little fog in London," said Ludlow, anxious to defend his beloved city in the presence of a foreigner. "The Mediterranean is most agreeable for a holiday, but I should hate to live anywhere but London."

"It's all right for you; you've made your way and you can sit back and enjoy it. I'm still struggling to get a decent practice at the Bar. I have to save up all the year for a holiday like this, and when I get back there may not be any work."

He looked gloomily at the ruins of the dessert. Ludlow, who considered himself to be far from having made his way fully in his own profession but did not worry about it, wondered at this flash of self-revelation from the young man who had hitherto seemed so smooth and superior. Was it perhaps that he had come near to money on this cruise, and had seen it withdraw? Certain observations and hints began to form into a pattern.

"Don't worry, son," Grossheim said. "The best things in life are free." He took out a large cigar.

"Not my best things. I intend to get on, and I intend to have money." Penge smiled, and changed as suddenly back to his normal mood.

Ludlow decided that he liked Rupert Penge better when he was being honestly acquisitive than when, as now, he started talking about fast sports cars and the fast girls who went in them. Leaving the other two to be enthusiastic about technical terms, he was free to watch David Acton come back to his table. Acton's face was set and strained. He sat down and said something quietly to Elizabeth, who compressed her lips and seemed worried. Theresa laughed, as if her father had just made a good joke.

The saloon was beginning to empty. Adrian Mallaby had not come back. A somnolent feeling was taking the place of previous animation. It seemed like a good time to escape, leaving Grossheim and Penge to their exchange of views. Ludlow excused himself politely and got up, brushing away the crumbs which he had somehow spread over his clothes in the course of the meal. He was near to freedom, and the cool solitude of the deck. Too late! Julie West was at his side, her face shining slightly from the heat of the saloon and the exertions of dinner.

"Did you enjoy your meal?" Ludlow asked with a summons to his reserve of politeness.

"It was swell. I couldn't eat half of it, because I just didn't have the appetite. And those stewards are so friendly, they get quite upset if you don't eat every course."

"Never mind, you did better than your cabin-companion."

"Yes, I think I'll go and see if Diana wants anything more. Maybe she'd like to come up on deck now that I can give her company. I guess she doesn't want to see too much of her family. It's sort of embarrassing in a way, but it does give me a lovely friend to talk to. You can get lonely by yourself on a big boat like this."

She trotted away leaving Ludlow to reflect on loneliness. It was wrong, he thought, to condemn the eager prattle of Julie West or the heavy humour of Adrian Mallaby. All people were lonely, and their sadness was that they reached out of their loneliness in so many different ways and seldom made contact. He leaned over the rail and watched the water shining far below. The darkness had fallen quickly while they were at dinner, and the stars gleamed more brightly than in England, veiled only momentarily as smoke from the funnel drifted across the view. Tomorrow would be another quiet day of sun and sea. It was the sort of life that seemed as if it could go on for ever. Here, where there was no sight of land but only the fluidity of endless motion, a little community was formed that might have had no contact with any other reality. Its loves and its hates were turned in among themselves, and there was no escape. This night at least, there was peace.

Ludlow turned away from the rail. A little farther along the deck, Rupert Penge was standing alone too, watching his own visions of fulfilled ambitions taking shape on the waves. Adrian Mallaby walked past, the complete seaman manifested in his self-conscious roll along the smooth and even deck. From the pantry came the clatter of plates.

He decided to go and collect his pipe and a book. Then a quiet corner of the bar might be found for the rest of the evening. Mercifully, there was no organized jollity this time. Also there was little danger of being accosted by Julie, since her cabin was on the other side of the ship. No doubt she and Diana would be talking animatedly, as women always seemed to do after forty minutes' parting from each other. He had only to slip through the foyer and all would be well.

He came to the bottom of the main stairway. A frenzied hand seized him, a face with mouth and eyes rounded in terror looked up into his.

"Please come with me," Julie said. "Something awful's happened to Diana."

— 5 —

The next few minutes had the quality of a dream, though the evidences of reality were only too palpable. Burrows had left his watchful post behind the desk when Julie appeared, and he now followed her back. The cabin which she was sharing with Diana was at the end of the corridor, well forward. Its open door faced them as they hurried towards it, running along the soft carpet that allowed no sound of urgency to echo back. In the doorway of the next cabin on one side, Cornelia Grossheim was standing, clutching a bright dressing-gown about her and demanding to know what all the noise was for. They ignored her and went into the cabin at the end.

It was a good cabin, well-furnished and designed to use every inch of space without giving any sense of crowding. Instead of the tiered berths of the cheaper cabins, there were two beds. One was by the wall to the left of the door as they came in. The other was under the porthole in the far wall and Diana Acton was lying on it. Like Cornelia, she was wearing a dressing-gown. But Cornelia's gown was bright and ugly, whereas Diana's was plain and obviously expensive. Cornelia was continuing to talk loudly, and Diana was not talking at all. She lay back awkwardly on the bed, her long legs hanging over on to the floor. Her face was twisted and blue.

A small table by her bed held a bowl of fruit, a glass jug nearly full of orange-coloured liquid and a plate with a fruit-knife. A glass tumbler was on the carpet a little way from the bed. Another table, at the other side of the cabin, bore a bottle of sherry and two glasses.

"Don't touch anything," Ludlow said.

Neither Julie nor Burrows showed any desire to touch anything, or indeed to come any farther than the door. Cornelia's protests and curiosity had now brought her to join them, and she peered at the bed where Diana lay. She fell suddenly silent and clutched the door for support. Ludlow looked away from the bed and tried to control his nausea. Then a voice said, quietly and as if amused,

"Is she dead?"

Theresa had come up unnoticed, so that they all started when she spoke. She stood, apparently self-possessed and mildly interested in the scene, ignoring Julie's attempts to turn her away from what she had to see.

"I'm afraid she is," Ludlow said gently.

Theresa laughed. She did not laugh loudly, not even in any way that could be called malicious or unfeeling. She simply laughed politely, as if a faintly amusing remark had been made in the course of conversation.

"Has she been poisoned?" she asked.

"That's impossible to say. I think you'd better fetch your parents." Ludlow, long accustomed to youthful gaucheries and apparent insensitivity, felt himself shocked, and troubled as if by an inhuman presence.

Theresa shrugged and went away. Ludlow turned to Burrows, who had done nothing but stand with his mouth open.

"Is there a doctor on the ship?" Ludlow asked.

"All cruise-ships carry a qualified doctor. Treatment is free, except in the case of ailments and injuries contracted before coming on board." Burrows seemed to take some pleasure in reciting his extract from the official information.

"Fetch him."

Giving Ludlow a look which suggested that this was not the way for passengers in the less expensive cabins to address the Cruise Director, Burrows moved reluctantly towards the telephone which was on the dressing-table.

"Don't touch that," Ludlow said sharply. "Perhaps Mrs. Grossheim will allow you to use the telephone in her cabin, which seems to be adjacent to this one."

This personal reference was too much for Cornelia, who collapsed into hysterical sobs and demands for Joseph. Julie took charge of her and led her away, with a calm sympathy which favourably impressed Ludlow. Burrows followed, like a desperate sheep-dog.

His back to the bed, Ludlow waited until Theresa came back with David and Elizabeth.

"They're glad it's happened," she announced.

"Shut up, you little fool," said David savagely. "What exactly is wrong?"

"I'm afraid your sister is dead," Ludlow said.

"That's impossible. She was all right before dinner."

"It looks as if she's been poisoned. I can't give a definite opinion, but I should say that it was some form of cyanide."

The effect of this on the Acton family was remarkable. Theresa laughed again. David and Elizabeth went pale and both recoiled as if Ludlow had said something deeply obscene. Yet their reaction seemed to have little in it of horror and less of pity. It was rather as if they were afraid.

"Where did she get it?" David said with an effort.

"I've no idea of the source of the poison. Perhaps you can answer that better than I can."

"What the devil do you mean?" There was anger now, mingled with the fear.

"Why, Mr. Acton, she was your sister. I am here only through a chance encounter with her companion. Perhaps we'd better wait for the doctor before we say any more."

The doctor was a red-faced, elderly man, whom Ludlow had seen regularly in the bar and had taken to be an officer off duty. He was pulling his white uniform straight as he came in, and making no attempt to conceal the alcoholic effect of his breath. Many years of dealing with mild sunstroke and indigestion had left him uncertain in the presence of crisis. This was something different from the rich old women who wanted to feel important and interesting; different even from the occasional sailor with a finger crushed in a winch. The doctor struggled to recover the years of training long ago, the worse years of an unsuccessful practice from which the sea had at last released him. He went over to the bed and began his examination. The others watched silent.

"She's dead, there's nothing I can do," the doctor said at last, getting up and dusting his knees.

"How long?" Ludlow shot the question at him as if dealing with a particularly inattentive student.

"I couldn't say."

"Surely you haven't forgotten how to determine the time of death."

"Well, really—oh, perhaps half an hour. It's not so easy to tell, you know."

"It's important to be as certain as we can. You must realize that this is not an accidental death. What would you say has happened?"

"She's been poisoned. It looks like some form of cyanide."

"We don't want any fuss." It was David Acton who spoke, looking at Ludlow with something less than admiration. "Diana's taken poison—she always was a nervy type and it's no good pretending I'm surprised. Let's leave it at that."

"I'm afraid we can't leave it at that, Mr. Acton. This is a case of violent death and it requires a full investigation. What we have to do is to make sure that the police have all the evidence that they need."

It must be admitted that Ludlow likes to occupy the centre of the scene and that he is apt to show off about his previous association with cases of murder.

"Can't you respect the feeling of the family?" David said.

"I am sure that the truth will do no harm to anyone's feelings—except those of the murderer."

Elizabeth shrieked at the word, and Theresa continued to look sullenly amused. David went pale and then red, and started to protest. Ludlow ignored him and turned back to the doctor.

"Doesn't your professional training make it clear to you that this is a case for the police?" he asked.

"It's nothing to do with me," said the doctor, looking like a man who feels that circumstances have treated him most unkindly. "You'd better talk to the Officer of the Watch."

He indicated a very young man, cleanly pink of face and white of uniform, who had been standing for some time in the doorway without anyone noticing him. Ludlow pounced on this new ally.

"Will you please be so good as to have this cabin locked and guarded until we reach the next bit of land—where is it?" he demanded.

"Malta, sir—the day after tomorrow," said the officer.

"Quite so. Now I want you to make sure that nothing in this cabin is disturbed. Nobody is to enter or leave it, after the body has been taken away for the doctor's post-mortem examination. Is that clear?"

"I shall have to get permission from the Captain, sir," said the officer; while the doctor seemed to be looking round in the hope that someone was going to produce a bottle of whiskey for him.

"Goodness me, is nobody able to act on this ship without reference to somebody else? It's as bad as a university. Well, ask the Captain, then. I suppose he will have to get permission from the Admiral and eventually the whole thing will be referred to the Prime Minister and we shall get nothing done at all."

During this general condemnation, the young officer had come right into the cabin and seen Diana's face. His pink face became white and he ceased giving attention to Ludlow, who therefore turned back to the doctor.

"You have the facilities for a post-mortem?" he asked.

"I haven't done a post-mortem for years. Surely that can wait until we get to port?" The doctor seemed almost plaintive. Ludlow had proved, not for the first time, that the best way to get authority is to assert it.

"It is essential that you should at least recover the contents of the stomach, and preserve them for analysis. Kindly have the body taken to your surgery and do what the situation demands. If you fail in this, you will be in trouble with Scotland Yard, the British Medical Association and the Editor of the *Lancet*. Now let me see, what else is there?"

"Everything's under control, Mr. Ludlow. You've no need to worry." It was Burrows who now tried to get the ship's privileges restored where they belonged.

"I'm not in the least worried. I think you'd better turn your attention to finding another cabin for Miss West."

Julie West, having left the moaning Cornelia in the care of Joseph, now returned as if on a cue and took up Ludlow's theme.

"Oh, Mr. Burrows, I couldn't sleep here tonight—I just couldn't. Please find me somewhere else."

"The passenger accommodation is fully booked," Burrows said mechanically. "Still, I'll see what I can do."

"Now let me see," Ludlow said as if anxious to wind up a dull committee as soon as possible, "what else is there? Oh yes."

He regained the attention of the young officer, who had by now recovered himself and was looking efficient again.

"Have you any means of communication with the land?" Ludlow asked. "Perhaps there is some kind of wireless that you use for the purpose?"

"We've got radio and radio-telephone links of course."

"Then please ask the man who looks after the wireless to tell Scotland Yard what has happened. You say we shall be at Malta the day after tomorrow. Fortunately that is a British possession—at least I think it still is, but one can never be sure nowadays. If it stays so for the next forty-eight hours, there will be no problem about getting the investigating detectives on board. What time do we get there?"

"About six a.m.," the officer said helplessly.

"A most unhealthy hour. But I have noticed that police officers work at strange times. That is all, then."

"It isn't necessary," David Acton said.

"I think it is. This is a British ship and we are making for a British port. It will be very awkward for everybody if we don't do what is right. Isn't that so?" he asked everyone impartially.

"This is going to be fun," said Theresa.

"I'm not sure if I have the proper facilities," said the doctor.

"I'll have to ask the Captain," said the Officer of the Watch.

It was midnight before Ludlow stopped walking to and fro on the deck and went below. The ship seemed very quiet. Every cabin was closed and presented a blank door which could not be blamed for anything or drawn into investigations. Diana's body had been removed for unwilling examination by the ship's doctor. Outside her cabin at the end of the corridor, a sailor stood on guard. From the ship's radio room, invisible under the gazing stars, waves of sound crackled from the Mediterranean to London and back again. Like the sad messengers of Greek tragedy, they carried news of sudden and violent death.

— 6 —

Morning came up through a mist which clung to the superstructure of the *Inquirer,* dripped off the rails, and generally made everything look like a ghostly ship and a phantom crew sailing out of an old legend. Anyone who liked to observe Nature with an eye that connected her moods with the human situation would have found the scene most appropriate. But the few sailors who moved as shadows through the mist seemed concerned with nothing but their appointed tasks; and by the time the first passengers were stirring, there was sunshine again and a clear sky.

News spreads fast through the small community of a ship, where the truth that no man is an island is made more observable than in the open society on land. There is no escape from the potential menace, whether it is fire, plague or sudden death. The ancient terrors were stirred, but were stilled again by the warm sun, the polite service of breakfast, the clean efficiency of the whole vessel. Passengers learned that a woman had died on the previous evening, but the Captain's orders had been so prompt and so well observed that there were few to whisper the word "Murder."

Ludlow was not up in time to see the morning mist, but he was up a great deal earlier than is usual with him. The deck was still damp from its daily wash when he found a chair and thankfully breathed the fresh sea breeze. His burst of activity after dinner, buoyed up by the demands of the crisis, had left him feeling weary and undecided. With one of his moods of self-criticism, he blamed himself for seeing murder where there might be none. Yet there could be no other explanation. Diana Acton had not been the kind of woman to kill herself, certainly not by the agonizing and distorting means of cyanide. And poison did not get dropped accidentally into jugs of orange juice—certainly not on a well-run ship like this. No, the gathering clouds of the past few days had broken; and now it was necessary to take some action before it was too late. There was a murderer on board, one who might strike again at anyone who seemed to menace his safety. Besides, the value of evidence tended to diminish as time passed after a crime. That was something which his previous association with the police had taught him. It was time to start.

Although the news had cast a slight gloom over breakfast, the upper deck was already beginning to take on its normal appearance. A great deal of bare flesh, varying in its fitness to be seen by others, was being disposed in places where the sun would strike it and give the tan which proved the boast of a Mediterranean holiday. The little swimming-pool splashed as its surface was broken by young divers and by those old enough and fat enough to know better. A bright rubber ball bounced wetly among the sun-bathers. Yet one who knew what to look for could detect that all was not as it had been. Theresa Acton had her usual expression under her usual make-up, but she sat alone and watched Rupert Penge, who had a book and appeared not to be noticing anything. David Acton stood at the stern of the ship, gripping the rail and looking fixedly at the white track across the water. Adrian Mallaby, bulging in too-small swimming trunks, flopped in and out of the pool without any sign of his usual flippant cheerfulness.

There was nothing to be gained here at present. Ludlow heaved himself from the chair and ambled off to the next deck. There were two people with whom he needed to talk. Julie West was still in her cabin, sleeping after the tablets which the doctor had given her. Elizabeth was probably somewhere more accessible, taking charge of everything on behalf of the family as she was accustomed to do. Ludlow went into the small writing-room which opened off the main lounge.

Elizabeth was there, sitting at one of the two tables and staring at a piece of paper in front of her, Ludlow loomed up at her side and then made a noise which he intended to express sympathy, surprise, readiness to withdraw and even greater readiness to help. Fortunately, Elizabeth wanted to be helped.

"I'm trying to write some cables to our friends and family," she explained. "There aren't any very near relatives, but there are a lot of people who'll expect to be told. What shall I say?"

"Well, I don't know," said Ludlow, finding even his powers of speech inadequate to this request. "Better make them as short as possible and send letters later."

"I suppose so. But it seems so awful to have to say that Diana killed herself. 'Suicide' is a horrid word to send in a cable."

"It is indeed, but there's no need to use it. The word for what has happened is even more horrid, and that had better be left until we know more. Just say that she died suddenly."

"I can't think why she did it. We were all so happy at lunch that afternoon. There was nothing in her manner to suggest that she was going to kill herself."

She did not seem to have heard Ludlow, who decided that it was time for shock treatment.

"Mrs. Acton, your sister-in-law did not kill herself," he said. "And what is more, *you know it.*"

Elizabeth looked up at him, startled yet perhaps relieved as well.

"Yes, I suppose I have known it all the time," she said. "I didn't want to think about it. She was murdered, wasn't she?"

"I'm afraid there's little doubt of that. But why were you so reluctant to face it?"

"Because I'm frightened—terribly frightened."

"Frightened of what?"

"I don't want to talk about it."

"Mrs. Acton," Ludlow said, with the sudden and unexpected gentleness which is as characteristic of him as his brusqueness, "you will have to talk about it quite soon. Since I am uninvolved, you may find it easier to talk to me first. But please yourself, and tell me to go away if you prefer."

He looked at her with his firm but kindly grey eyes, until she seemed to drop her resistance and become bonelessly weak on her chair. She motioned him to sit down next to her.

"Now tell me why you are frightened," he said.

"Because of the money—and because of the poison which was used."

"Try to be more explicit," said Ludlow, with donnish encouragement as if to an inarticulate student. "Money in itself does not frighten anyone. Quite the reverse, in fact. You told me that your sister-in-law had inherited a great deal of money. Who will get it now?"

"David. She never made a will, and it will all come to him as the nearest relative. Now do you see why I'm frightened?"

"I can see why suspicion might fall on your husband, which is not necessarily the same thing, if he can prove his innocence. You were, however, in need of money?"

"We aren't starving or anything like that. But David certainly needs it for the business."

"Quite so. Now, remembering that I am not a policeman, and that the sooner we get at the truth the better it will be for everyone, will you tell me how you and your husband passed the time between say, seven o'clock yesterday evening and the time you came to your sister-in-law's cabin."

"Well, we were on the upper deck all afternoon. You remember that I came and talked to you for a while. After that, I went back and sat with David on the other side of the deck. We didn't move at all until about half past seven, when it was time to go down and change for dinner. We went straight to our cabin, and straight to the dining-saloon afterwards."

"Had your sister-in-law already gone to her cabin when you left the deck?"

"She was sitting with that American girl most of the time—they were on that little bit of deck at the back of the ship. I didn't see them go, but I didn't notice them there either when we did, so I suppose they must have."

"Quite," said Ludlow, disentangling this last bit of syntax with difficulty and disapproval. "What do you think of Miss West?"

"She seems a very nice girl. I haven't seen an awful lot of her but Diana obviously liked her. And she certainly helped us in sorting out that trouble over the cabins."

"Good. Now, your cabin is, I think, adjacent to that of your sister-in-law, and opposite the one occupied by Mr. and Mrs. Grossheim."

"Yes. Diana had the cabin at the end of the corridor, as you saw last night. David and I are on the right, as you face towards it, and the Grossheims are opposite us. Then Theresa moved into the cabin on our other side, with the French woman."

"I see. And who has the cabin opposite your sister-in-law?"

"Rupert Penge. And that fat man who had a row with him in the dance—I can't remember his name."

This was interesting, Ludlow thought. Rupert Penge and Adrian Mallaby were in the came cabin. In spite of the hostility that had grown up between them over Diana, they were forced into continual proximity. He brooded on this for a time.

"It would seem then," he said at last, "that you must

have seen the tray which was brought to Miss Acton's cabin."

"Oh yes. The stewardess had just put it down when we were coming out for dinner. David asked her who it was for, and she said that Diana had sent for it and said that it was to be left outside her door."

"That didn't surprise you?"

"Not at all. Diana was always inclined to miss meals because she was afraid of getting fat. If she'd lived to be my age and looked after a family, she'd have stopped bothering."

Elizabeth laughed, mirthlessly and with bitterness, so that for a moment Ludlow thought that he could see where Theresa had got some at least of her character. But the respectable, matronly mask was replaced at once.

"Did you go up to dinner immediately?"

"Yes—well, in a minute or two. I went and told Theresa to hurry up. She said that she wouldn't be last, because Diana was always late."

"But, no doubt, you said that Miss Diana Acton was not having dinner?"

"Yes, I said she was having a tray."

Elizabeth seemed to regret this as soon as she said it. Ludlow apparently took no notice, but gazed out of the window and watched the sea flickering away to the horizon. The sun was higher, and the shouts and splashes of the upper deck came faintly to where they were sitting. The steady pulse of the engines made him feel as if he were sitting on a comfortable hotel built over a power-station. He regretted the time being spent away from the sunshine, that precious commodity which has to be pursued so expensively by the people of these damp islands. He sighed, but his next question came out incisively.

"Why did your husband leave the dining-saloon during dinner yesterday evening?"

"Never mind." Elizabeth seemed agitated, and turned her face away.

"I don't mind at all," Ludlow said comfortably, "but the police will. They'll want to know exactly where he went and why he went there."

"David won't tell them. He hates being questioned and he's very independent about what he does."

"That will be unwise of him. However. Perhaps you can and will tell me something else. You say that you were just leaving your cabin when the tray was being left for your sister-in-law. Can you remember if anyone else was in the corridor at the time?"

Elizabeth looked relieved, but perhaps a little suspicious at the change of subject. She frowned thoughtfully, then shook her head.

"There was nobody else," she said. "The corridor was empty."

"Were any of the other cabin doors open?"

"Well—Theresa's wasn't, because I spoke to her through it. And the Grossheim's door was closed. The cabin where Rupert Penge is—I think—yes, the door was open a little."

"Could you tell who, if anyone, was inside?"

"No. I didn't take any notice, and anyway it was only open a little. But I see what you're getting at: who could have known that Diana was having a tray? Yes, that's important, isn't it? If we could only be sure who was listening——"

"Mrs. Acton, why did you say, a few minutes ago, that you were afraid because of the poison that was used?"

Ludlow's voice cut across Elizabeth's excited desire to get away from questions about her own family. She faltered and stopped, then looked away. She stared at the half-written cablegrams on the desk, and it seemed that a defeated woman sat there at last. Ludlow pitied her, but his lean face showed nothing.

"I oughtn't to have told you that," she said quietly.

"Perhaps not, but you did. What did you mean?"

"Nothing. Well—oh, I suppose it will all come out when the police start asking everyone questions."

"I'm sure it will. Why not tell me now?"

"Theresa had cyanide in her cabin."

She glared at Ludlow for a moment as she spat out the words, then slumped back and stared at the desk. Ludlow, always proud of not appearing surprised, swallowed hard and decided that he was not so good at it as he had thought. The gleam of the sea outside was dazzling, as he took out his pipe and scraped it busily while he considered how to frame his next question without frightening Elizabeth into complete silence.

"In what kind of container did she keep it?" he asked, as prosaically as if they were discussing ways of storing tobacco.

"It was in a tin." Elizabeth seemed reassured, as he had hoped.

"And where did she get it?"

"From a chemist, in London. She just went in and said she wanted to destroy a wasps' nest, and signed the register quite normally. It seems all wrong to me that a girl should be able to get it so easily. Of course, the chemist knew David—it's a shop just by the works—so there was no difficulty."

"But what was her purpose in bringing it on board this ship?" Ludlow asked, feeling that the conversation was becoming distinctly unreal.

"She just brought it for fun."

"Fun!" There are many former students who would have loved to see that Ludlow could be really shaken out of his composure. "Well really, it's hardly my idea of fun, and I have never supposed myself wanting in a sense of humour. I have known students, when charged with some particularly violent and dangerous action, allege that they were only having a joke with their friends. On such occasions, I have always asked them what they do with their enemies. Have I perhaps found the answer?"

"You don't understand Theresa, Mr. Ludlow." Elizabeth seemed at ease again. "She wouldn't even consider hurting anyone. But she does like to show off and draw attention to herself. Only about a year ago, she sent her own obituary notice to the local newspaper; but it was worded in such a peculiar way that they made inquiries and didn't print it. You see, it gave her pleasure just to have that tin with her and hope people would ask questions about it. She wrote 'Cyanide' in big letters on the label, so of course everyone thought it was just a joke and took no notice of it. I don't think even David believed her. I did, but it's much easier in the long run to let her have her own way. But I worried about it and I told her she oughtn't to keep it, in case it did harm by accident. Last night she told me that she threw it overboard, after we left Piraeus. So you see, it wasn't her poison that was used."

"I only hope they weren't fishing for any part of our dinner at the time. However, it's as well that she did. But you'd better tell the story when the police come, because they'll be much more suspicious if they hear about it from somebody else who may have seen the tin in her cabin."

With this final piece of advice, Ludlow took his way out of the writing-room. As he emerged again into the sunshine, he meditated on the perils of marrying and having a family. It seemed strange that an apparently ordinary and rather dull pair like Elizabeth and David should have produced anything so alarming as Theresa. Yet the strain had been in Diana too, a continual posing that seemed like a mannered flirtation with death. And who could say from what tormented ancestor that dark stain had come? He found a chair on the promenade deck, on the shaded side forsaken by the sun-worshippers. he leaned back and closed his eyes, searching for a thread of sense in the tortuous pattern which Elizabeth had just offered him. A familiar voice broke into his thoughts.

"May I sit and talk with you for a while, Mr. Ludlow?"

Not waiting for any reply, Joseph P. Grossheim lowered himself into the next chair. He was wearing an alarming shirt decorated with blue flowers which would have created difficulties of classification for a learned botanist. His grey shorts revealed knees that were not meant for revelation. Ludlow groaned almost audibly, but then reflected that he might profit by this offer to talk. He smiled, though somewhat coldly; Grossheim needed no stronger encouragement.

"I've left Cornelia down in our cabin," he explained. "She ain't feeling too good, after all that bother last evening. Seeing the poor girl laid out on the bed was just too much for her. Cornelia is very sensitive."

"I hope she will recover her spirits soon," Ludlow said.

"Oh, she'll be fine in an hour or two. She just thought she didn't want to come up on deck too early. Mr. Ludlow, this is a terrible thing."

Grossheim looked with a grave, senatorial face, but there was a nervous twitch at the side of his mouth. This was clearly yet another source of information to be tapped. Ludlow prodded delicately.

"It is indeed," he said. "One person on this ship must be realizing just how terrible, and wishing that it could be revoked. Yet how can one hope to enter the mind of a murderer? Does the same conscience stir in him that would torment you and me, or is he already beyond repentance before he strikes?"

"You guess it's murder, then?" Grossheim shifted uneasily in his chair.

"I guess nothing. It is the only possible deduction that can be reached in the circumstances."

"Then the cops will be coming on board to grill everyone."

"I have no doubt that police officers will embark at Malta and carry out an investigation."

"Yeah. Tell me something—are your British cops kind of brutal?"

"My own impression of the police has been most favourable. My friend Inspector Montero is a highly intelligent man and far from brutal. He carries out his work with a natural compassion which must sometimes be hard to maintain. Of course, he lacks an academic training and is inclined to jump to conclusions. I have had to help him out on more than one occasion. Still, he is well read and has a true critical sense——"

"That's swell," cut in Grossheim, who was unused to Ludlow and was rapidly getting lost. "I only hope we get a good guy sent out here as well. Because the questions are going to be a bit delicate for some folk."

"Really?" Ludlow looked all innocence. "Who do you think has anything to hide?"

"Well, not anything to hide, maybe. But on these boats, folk may act up a bit different to what they would at home. I mean, it's a vacation, and you don't have to think all the time what Main Street might be saying about it. But then a thing like this happens, and a lot of things get dragged out—things that have nothing to do with the crime, but might look bad if the tecs get the wrong idea."

"I'm not sure that I follow you, Mr. Grossheim. What sort of thing have you in mind?" Ludlow's nose was almost quivering with excitement.

"Well, I'll give you an example of what happened to a friend of mine when he was on vacation. He's a good guy, a regular fellow, but he ain't no pussy foot either. He likes to have a bit of fun, no doing harm to anyone, you understand me. One time, he made a pass at a dame who was staying up at the same place in the mountains. Next day, she was found dead. The cops came in, said it was homicide. This guy didn't know what to do when they started going over his movements. He hadn't done a thing, but he didn't think it'd look too good if he said he'd stepped a bit out of the way. Other hand, if he didn't tell and they found out, it might look bad for him. What do you reckon he ought to have done?"

"He ought to have told the police everything he knew about the dead woman and his relations with her."

"Yeah, natch. Still, you can see that it was kind of awkward for him."

"No doubt. What bearing has this unfortunate incident on the present situation?"

"Just academic interest, Professor. I was curious to know what you'd say."

The look which Ludlow now turned on Grossheim was academic in quite another way. It had the impression of a man who has mislaid his magnifying-glass and is trying to see the details of something small and rather unattractive. Grossheim wriggled, opened his mouth and shut it soundlessly.

"If you really want my advice," Ludlow said severely, "you'd better tell me exactly when and how you—er—made a pass at Diana Acton."

"Why, Mr. Ludlow—I've just been telling you a story about another guy. You've no need to think it was me. I mean, I wouldn't do a thing like that. I mean, I—well, O.K., O.K., you're too sharp, I guess. So I did have a bit of fun, no harm. But I never killed her."

"Tell me. Or if not, at least be sure to tell the police when they come on board. For your own sake, as well as in the furtherance of truth."

"I'll tell you; it wasn't anything so awful. Second night out, I got talking to Diana up here on the deck—right about where we are now. Talked about the stars and the sea, and all how romantic it was. We found we had cabins right near to each other. After a while, she said she felt cold, so I suggested we go in the bar for a drink. She said, why didn't we go for a drink to her cabin. Which we did. No harm in that, I guess."

"None, I'm sure. I take it that your wife was elsewhere at the time."

"Natch. Cornelia was talking with some ladies in the lounge. I went down with Diana, sat around while she fixed me a drink. Then she came over to me and started getting quite amorous. I can't say I objected. I mean, it may not be quite right, but who's hurt if the wife never knows? Anyway, we never got far because Miss Julie West came in—she was changing over her cabin to be with Diana, and had to move her things. So we broke it up."

"And did you—ah—repeat the experiment?"

"Sure tried. Next day, Diana was coming out of her cabin just when I was going to mine. I said hello, and sort of put my arm around her. She pushed me off, like I was a snake, and started bawling me out. Then Cornelia came along looking for me. That really finished it. Women are queer creatures, Mr. Ludlow."

"So the poets have often remarked. I hope this did not cause a serious quarrel between yourself and your wife."

"Cornelia cooled off after a while. I never told her what had happened the night before—she was mad enough at me as it was."

"Natch. I mean, quite so."

"You guess I ought to tell the cops all this?"

"It would be as well, if they ask you any questions. They're almost certain to do so, since your cabin is so near the one where the murder took place. But I think you can trust them not to tell your wife more than she needs to know."

"That's swell. Thank you, Mr. Ludlow, you've taken quite a load off my mind."

Grossheim heaved himself from his chair and wandered off, leaving Ludlow to develop a few ideas while looking prim about shipboard morals.

When he eventually went down to wash before lunch, Ludlow was surprised to hear his name called as he was crossing the main foyer. Behind his customary desk, Burrows stood with a top-price, Boat-Deck-passenger smile. Behind the smile, there was anxiety and an unexpected diffidence. Always ready to be the centre of attention, Ludlow crossed to him at once.

"I was hoping to see you, Mr. Ludlow," Burrows said, "but of course I couldn't think of disturbing you on deck, this lovely morning."

This did not seem to need any answer, and Ludlow gave none. Burrows smiled hopefully for a few moments and then went on.

"We've been in touch with the owners, in London. Indeed, there's been a great deal of communication both ways since the unfortunate affair last night."

"Ah yes, I believe that much can be done by modern methods. One might conjecture idly about what would have happened in history if news had been sent more quickly. For instance——"

"The police have been informed," Burrows said, seeing Ludlow disappearing down a digression. "Two men from Scotland Yard are coming on board tomorrow when we reach Malta."

"Very proper and commendable speed by everyone." Ludlow wondered why he was being favoured with all this information. He was soon enlightened.

"It seems," Burrows went on, "that the Inspector in charge of the case asked to see our passenger-list, and went through it carefully. He noticed your name, and asked a few questions about you. Apparently he is a friend of yours. Inspector Montero."

Ludlow looked pleased. It seemed that the curiosity which had caused him to start making inquiries on his own was going to be rewarded. Though the circumstances which had first brought them together had not been happy, there had grown up a mutual respect and liking between himself and the Inspector. They shared a love of English literature, and a tendency to quote from it at unlikely moments which was the despair of Montero's sergeant, Jack Springer. Ludlow resolved to learn all he could that day, so that he could give his friend something to think about when he arrived. His meditation was broken when Burrows spoke again.

"It seems that the Inspector spoke very highly of you. So no doubt you will be giving him some help in his investigations."

"Perhaps," Ludlow said.

"I trust that you have enjoyed your cruise so far."

"Very much." Ludlow wondered where this was leading.

"May I express the hope that you will be able to put in

a word for the line, and for the cruise staff in particular? I'm sure you will agree that this kind of thing could do great damage to our reputation if it was reported in the wrong way. Will you do what you can to help?"

"I shall do what I can to arrive at the truth, so far as Inspector Montero may ask for my help," said Ludlow, feeling pompous but enjoying himself.

"Oh, of course, we all want to arrive at the truth, don't we? But it's so difficult to know which facts may be relevant. That's why I was wondering—do you think I ought to say anything about Miss Acton's jewels?"

"What is there to say about them?"

"Well, she had a good deal of jewellery on board—some of it is very expensive. She wisely deposited it in the ship's safe. The line is not responsible for property lost in cabins or public rooms, though we take every precaution to ensure security."

Ludlow looked at him encouragingly, but without comment.

"But yesterday," Burrows went on, "just before lunch—about this time—Miss Acton came and took out all her jewellery. I thought it unwise of her, but it was not my business to comment."

"That may be important. I don't know. But you certainly ought to tell Inspector Montero. Is the jewellery in her cabin now?"

"I don't know. We left everything as it was, and the cabin is locked. It seemed to be a circumstance that ought to be mentioned."

Burrows coughed, and braced himself for his real announcement.

"The fact is, Mr. Ludlow, that I should be glad not to be drawn too deeply into the investigations. You see, I did have a little—unpleasantness—with Miss Acton, soon after the cruise started."

"About her cabin? Yes, I heard something about that."

"Oh dear, it just shows how these things get around. She really was rather unreasonable, wanting to change her cabin immediately, when the ship was fully booked. She made such a fuss, but fortunately everything was resolved quite satisfactorily. But do you think this will be held against me?"

"I shouldn't think so for a moment. From what I gather, a good many people had unpleasantness of one sort or another with her."

"Thank you, Mr. Ludlow. It's a great relief to hear you say that. I'm sure that all our interests will be safe in your hands. And do let me know if there's anything I can do to make your holiday more enjoyable, in spite of what has happened."

"There is one thing——"

"Anything I can do, Mr. Ludlow, anything at all."

"I understand that we shall arrive at Malta very early in the morning. Inspector Montero is a man of unhealthy habits and has no respect for sleep. Please see that he does not come near me before nine o'clock."

— 7 —

Lunch that day, though admirable as ever in quality and service, was not very enjoyable. Ludlow's table in particular seemed to be under a little cloud of its own, rivalled in blackness only by the one which hung over the table where the Actons sat. Cornelia appeared for the meal, but she and Joseph said scarcely a word to each other or to anyone else: a silence so unusual in them that it seemed to forebode more trouble. Rupert Penge was talkative enough, but most of his words were directed towards finding out what Ludlow had been doing, and resenting it. He obviously regarded himself as the right man to take charge of things until the police arrived.

"I hear you've been asking questions," he said suddenly at a moment which caught Ludlow with his mouth full of lobster.

"It is the oldest and best method of learning the truth," Ludlow replied, swallowing quickly, "and one which my profession teaches me to do as thoroughly as possible."

"My profession is to ask questions too."

"And do you always reach the truth?"

"I try to see that justice is done. A barrister has to bring out the aspects of the case which are going to help his client."

"Perhaps that's where we differ on this matter. I have no client except a rather shabby old lady called Truth. You may have other interests."

Ludlow looked very pointedly across to where Theresa was sitting with her parents. As he had hoped, Rupert went red and then white, and savagely tore the remains of his roll. He sulked until almost the end of the meal.

"I think this case needs a lawyer to look after it," he said at last.

"I understand that a very able detective—a friend of mine as it happens—is coming on board tomorrow. I'm sure that he will do all that is necessary."

"That's just what I mean. I'm used to dealing with the police. They're quite good fellows, but they often go all out to get a conviction in spite of the evidence. If I have a good case to present to them, we may save a lot of time—and a lot of trouble for innocent people."

Ludlow smiled to himself at the thought of this young man trying to patronize Montero. He made a non-committal reply, and got up from the table. Before he could get to the door, he was stopped by a deferential cough from the white-coated figure of Harmer, the steward who served his table and the Actons.

"I hope you've enjoyed your meal, sir."

"Yes, thank you."

"I hope the service has been satisfactory. Please let me know if there's ever anything extra you need—I'll be happy to oblige you."

This was different from the competent but usually rather surly treatment that Harmer gave to his tables. Ludlow realized again how quickly news travels on a ship, and also what reflected glory can do to make life easier.

"I understand that the police Inspector who's coming on board at Malta is a friend of yours, sir. That being so, I wonder whether you might put in a good word for me, if it isn't asking too much."

"What sort of good word?" Ludlow asked, puzzled.

"In case anything gets said about the row I had with Miss Acton a couple of days ago. You must remember it, sir."

"I didn't notice anything," said Ludlow, who indeed usually applied himself to his food with an enthusiasm that excluded most outside noises.

"Well, she was dissatisfied with the service. We had a bit of delay in the pantry and she took exception to waiting. I'm afraid I spoke back, a bit out of turn maybe, but it made things just as awkward for us as it did for the passengers. Anyway she flew off, said she'd report me back in London and get me sacked. It didn't worry me too much—I can get a job in any ship—but it might make things look a bit dodgey."

"You mean, you might be thought to have a motive for killing her? But surely, you were up here before dinner and all through it, and she only had a tray sent down to her cabin."

"That's just it, sir. I prepared the tray, because she was on one of my tables. It could look bad for me, that poison in the drink. Will you speak up for me, sir?"

"I think we can trust Inspector Montero to get at the truth."

Ludlow went out of the saloon, feeling that his remarks were getting somewhat repetitive. However, his inquisitive spirit was aroused; and he had been irritated more than he cared to admit by the attitude of Rupert Penge. For once, therefore, he did not shrink when he saw Julie West bearing down on him. She looked drawn and frightened, with her eyes bulging moistly behind her glasses. She trotted up to Ludlow and began her recital.

"Oh, Professor, isn't this just too awful! Poor Diana sitting up here so happy yesterday afternoon and now she's dead, and in that horrible way. Who could have done a thing like that?"

"Perhaps we shall find out, with your help," Ludlow said, steering his important witness towards a chair. "I take it, from your remarks, that you do not think it was suicide?"

"Oh, no, why would Diana do that?"

"I don't think she did. Now, the Inspector who is going to investigate this case is known to me, and I may say that I have a great regard for his ability in these matters. I believe that it is important to recall everything that may have any bearing on the crime—for crime it certainly is, and of the most cruel and evil kind. Do you feel willing and able to tell me what you know, starting from yesterday afternoon?"

"Sure, I'll tell you anything. You've got that reliable sort of feeling, that makes a girl feel good."

Ludlow grunted, not with displeasure, and looked at the sea.

"Perhaps we could go back a little earlier in fact," he said. "Do you know whether Miss Acton did anything special just before lunch yesterday?"

"Oh yes, she went and got her jewels out of the safe where Mr. Burrows was keeping them for her."

"Have you any idea why she did that?"

"Not a guess. She just came into the cabin carrying a square box and said, 'These are my jewels—they're worth a lot of money,' or something like that, and put the box in her wardrobe."

"Could anyone else have heard her say that?"

"I don't see how. Maybe she still had the door open, though. Yes, I guess she had. Do you think someone murdered her to get her jewels?"

"I've no idea, but it seems a possibility. It depends on whether they are found intact when the cabin is opened tomorrow. By the way, I hope that Burrows found you somewhere satisfactory to sleep."

"Oh, he put me in a swell cabin, right up on the top deck. I didn't care much where it was, if I could only get away. But—say, why did he tell Diana that there was no empty cabin for her to go into when she wanted to change?"

"Because of the prevarication which is endemic among hotel receptionists, estate-agents and all who have the disposal of accommodation. Perhaps they like to feel their power, or perhaps they just don't want to be bothered with any changes. The English are particularly bad in this way, quite lacking the standards of service to be found in many countries—however. When did you next see Miss Acton, after you had gone to your respective tables for lunch?"

"We met up on the sun-deck, maybe half two. We just sat there and lazed in the sun for hours. Have you noticed how time just seems to slip by when you're at sea?"

"I have. It's really rather disconcerting. Did you stay there until it was time for dinner?"

"Yes, we did—at least, till it was time to go down and change."

"Did you go into the lounge for afternoon tea?"

"No, we didn't stir. Diana didn't want anything, and I just can't get into the British habit of drinking tea all the time. In the States, we drink a lot more coffee than you. I don't mind tea, though. I guess every Englishman likes to have tea."

"The practice varies," said Ludlow, who is as good at avoiding other people's digressions as he is bad about following his own. "So Miss Acton had nothing to eat or drink all the afternoon?"

"No, she didn't want anything. I went up and got myself some juice at the little bar they have on the sun-deck, but Diana had nothing."

"When did you leave the sun-deck?"

"About seven, I guess. I didn't notice. Diana said, why didn't we go and have a glass of sherry in the cabin while we changed. She had a few bottles there, and she liked taking a drink before meals. I'm not used to it, but I went along with her."

"Which reminds me, talking about drink—do you remember seeing your compatriot Mr. Grossheim in the cabin, the night you moved in?"

"Sure, he was there having a drink with Diana when I came in with my cases. I remember he seemed kind of agitated and not too pleased to see me. But he made some excuse and went out, just as soon as I came."

"Thank you. But to return to yesterday—you went to your cabin and both had sherry?"

"Yes. I took a shower first, and Diana poured out some sherry for me. She had a glass too—maybe she had one already while I was in the shower. I don't know."

"Could anyone possibly have come into the cabin while you were in the bathroom?"

"I don't think so. You can't hear very well with the water running but Diana and I were having a sort of shouted conversation most of the time. Anyway I got dressed, but Diana said she wasn't coming up to dinner. She said she'd have a shower, and telephone up for a tray."

"Did this strike you as at all surprising?"

"No, she'd missed meals before. She used to worry about her figure. They sure do give you big meals on this ship, but I'm always ready for them. Maybe I ought to worry about my figure a bit more."

She looked hopefully at Ludlow with these words. But as he did not respond she merely sighed and said, "Poor Diana, it doesn't matter to her any longer."

"Did she telephone while you were there?" Ludlow asked, pressing on relentlessly and refusing to be distracted.

"Well, no. She was standing over by the phone as if she was just going to use it. I went up on deck—and that was when I saw you, Professor. You remember—we had such a nice little chat before dinner."

"Yes, most agreeable. Then you went back to the cabin after dinner and found her dead."

"Yes, I just walked in, and she was lying on the bed, the way you saw her. It was so horrible—I'll never forget it, never."

"You will," Ludlow said, with his rare but true gentleness. "Things are forgotten very quickly. Which is a good reason for getting your recollections now. You'll have to tell the Inspector tomorrow, and it'll be easier for you if you've been through it already. Horror is best reduced by facing it."

"You're so kind." Julie sniffed into her handkerchief, while the *Inquirer* ploughed on towards Malta, carrying the poisoned body of Diana Acton along with all its living cargo.

"Now, think carefully," Ludlow said when she seemed to be a little recovered, "did you lock the cabin door when you left?"

"Why, no. There was no point with Diana staying there."

"Of course not. And was it still open when you returned after dinner?"

"Yes. I just turned the knob and went in."

"Was the tray on the table by the bed, as I saw it later?"

"I suppose so. I can't remember anything, but seeing Diana with that awful blue face. I just screamed and ran out."

"At least, it wasn't outside the door?"

"No, I'm sure of that."

"Thank you, Miss West. Go and sit in the sun and try to forget."

Julie lingered, as Ludlow had known she would.

"Is there anything else you would like to tell me?" he asked.

"No—that is—no, I guess there isn't."

Still she sat there and looked out over the rail, where the lightest white caps were breaking on the surface of the sea.

"Miss West," Ludlow said in his voice for slow-witted students, "something is worrying you. I should go so far as to say that something is frightening you. What is it?"

"There isn't anything really. It can't have anything to do with what happened to Diana, and I just don't know why I should feel worried about it either. But she wanted to invest a bit of money in the property I've inherited back at home. She said she liked to spread her money out and make it work for her, and she was interested in what I told her—seemed to think all that land was going to be worth an awful lot of money in a few years. I just don't know a thing about it, though maybe I'll have to learn now. But Diana knew all about investments and stocks and things: you'd never have thought it, would you? Anyway, she was going to speak with her lawyers in London and get their advice."

"Who else knew about this?"

"I think she said something to that fat man, Adrian Mallaby. She was getting pretty friendly with him, the last day or two. I don't like him—he frightens me."

"Why does he do that?"

"I don't know, that's the silly part of it. But I do feel frightened—not just of him, but of the whole thing. I've got an awful feeling that I was somehow partly to blame for Diana's death, and that whoever did it was going to be after me too. I just don't know."

"Don't worry," Ludlow said. "I'm sorry to have raised all these unpleasant things, but it was necessary. I'm sure you have nothing to worry about. But if you feel nervous, try not to be alone too much. Now I must think."

Julie accepted her dismissal and went, leaving Ludlow very thoughtful and not entirely happy. He found himself looking forward to Montero's arrival and the chance to exchange ideas. A vague anxiety about Julie nagged at him, was firmly rebuked but kept tugging at his sleeve. At last he got up and walked to the sun-deck.

The usual afternoon scene presented itself, with sprawling forms absorbing more sun than they would feel for the rest of the year. "Every man's death diminishes me," he murmured to himself, but this crowd did not seem in the least diminished. There were the same splashes and shrieks from the tiny pool, the same dim throb of the engines and the wash of the sea as a path was driven through it. This might have been the previous afternoon, or any afternoon in an endless summer of leisure and peace.

Ludlow was relieved, though annoyed at himself for worrying, to see Julie sitting quietly and apparently at ease with Elizabeth Acton. Theresa was with Rupert Penge, who no longer seemed sullen but laughed gaily as they threw a rubber ring to each other. Under their different veneers, Ludlow thought rather sadly, they each had still the weakness and the strength of youth. In all this trouble and suspicion, they showed so much to be pitied, and so much to be envied. In a shady corner, the Grossheims were sitting close together and talking in low voices. Cornelia's face was hard; Joseph looked both harassed and defiant, as he occasionally punctuated what appeared to be mainly a monologue. It looked like being a long punishment for a brief indiscretion.

Turning his back on them all and leaning over the rail, Ludlow thought of the land that was out of sight yet gave meaning to this emptiness of water. He thought again of the ships that had gone out, small and unguided, to prove that Man was the master of all things. He thought of the ships that had turned their prows towards Troy, to begin the legend that had grown to be more human truth than the undoubted chronicles of history. Yet before that moment of doom, and through the centuries ever since, there had been killing: murder as the means of attaining whatever men might desire. But out of what lust, or greed, or fear, had Diana Acton been subjected to agony and the ugliness of death? What time would reveal began to chill the shining afternoon.

Dinner was another difficult meal. Improved perhaps by exercise, perhaps by affection, Rupert Penge was his usual facetious but not disagreeable self. The Grossheims forced themselves to some kind of conversation, though Cornelia still had the appearance of a walking rat-trap, and Joseph looked as if he had not slept for a week. Harmer, never cheerful, now served the meal like a man already under sentence. Ludlow ate and drank well, but for once was glad when it was over. He had hoped for some more ideas, in the unguarded moments of eating, but he could learn nothing. A few people were anxious and fearful, while the majority of the passengers were enjoying themselves as if nothing had happened; but he had known this already.

He managed to avoid company during the dangerous

period just after dinner, when people were arranging their activities for the evening. He stood for a long time at the stern, watching the sea and thinking. Eventually he went into the bar, where a few couples were dancing in a shuffling and dismal sort of way, which seemed to give them adequate pleasure. Ludlow sat up by the bar and talked desultorily to the barman. After a few minutes his peace was broken by a large figure perching itself on the next stool.

"Well, well, if it isn't the amateur sleuth," said Adrian Mallaby. "What are you having, Sherlock?"

"I'm all right, thank you," Ludlow replied coldly.

"You'll need a bit of refreshment after asking all those questions. Have you got any juicy bits to tell your pals in the police tomorrow?"

"I don't know what you mean," Ludlow said. "I have learnt a few interesting facts, but no doubt Inspector Montero will soon learn them for himself. He is a clever man."

"Is he now? Then there's no harm in passing on a few hints."

"I think I ought to keep my information to myself. Anyway, you must understand that I have no authority in this matter, only an insatiable curiosity. And the more one teaches, the more one realizes what a lot there is to be learnt about the world."

"You're right there, old boy. Never too old to learn, I always say. Do you know the one about the old maid who—"

"For instance," Ludlow interrupted him, "I have learnt quite a lot today about investments and the prospects of certain American property."

Mallaby shifted uneasily on his stool and drank deeply. Then he wiped his mouth with his hand and returned to the attack, seeming to ignore Ludlow's last words.

"Don't you think it could be dangerous to get mixed up in this sort of thing? I mean, if there's a murderer on board, he might take a dim view of anyone who got too inquisitive. I'm not trying to frighten you, old boy, but they do say that where there's one murder there's often two."

"I don't think that any innocent person on this ship has anything to fear," Ludlow said, with more confidence than he felt at that moment.

"Hope you're right!" Mallaby swallowed his drink and went away, leaving Ludlow with the thought that yet another person was obviously not looking forward to Montero's arrival.

It may be that Ludlow sat too long at the bar and drank too much whiskey after a day in the sun. No doubt it also had something to do with his recent reflections on the Greek past, and his talk with Americans on the theme of murder. For whatever reason, he dreamed that night that he had been sent for review a modern version of Homer. It seemed to start something like this:

"'That guy Achilles sure had it coming to him,' quipped genial, balding Police Chief Agamemnon, as he burnished his automatic, the gift of many-arted Pallas. . . ."

— 8 —

The *Inquirer* was at rest in the Grand Harbour at Valetta before most of her passengers were awake. Anyone who had risen early for a first view of Malta could have seen two strangers being received on board with a kind of furtive deference which left some doubt whether their business was honourable or disreputable. One of them was of little more than medium height, with a close, fair moustache and deceptively gentle blue eyes. His voice was soft and bore a faint trace of the West Country when he greeted the Officer of the Watch. The other was tall and thin, his dark face bearing a serious expression that looked ready to break at any moment into laughter. Their dark suits contrasted with the current shipboard fashions, and they both had raincoats over their arms. Inspector Montero and Sergeant Springer of the C.I.D. had arrived from England.

After some hard work in Diana Acton's cabin, in the course of which several little packets were handed to a Maltese detective-constable who accompanied them, they went to look for Ludlow. They found him eating toast and admiring the great sweep of the bay as it could be seen through the windows of the saloon.

"Have you had breakfast?" he asked hospitably after rising and shaking hands.

"We had it on the plane, several hours ago," Montero answered. "I thought we'd better let you get your normal twelve hours' sleep. Well, you've managed to get yourself mixed up in another bit of trouble."

"I seem to be pursued by murders," Ludlow said sadly. "But I refuse to have my holiday interrupted in any way by what is apparently known as the crime wave. Quite appropriate for this case, really. Though the sea has mercifully been very calm indeed, which is more than can be said for the passions on board. Still, as I say, I have not allowed any of it to interfere with me."

"Come off it," said Montero, who knew his man by now. "You know that you've been asking questions like mad ever since it happened, and that you're bursting to tell us."

"If I happen to have picked up anything in conversation, I might repeat it if I did not feel it to be confidential. But this is not going to be an easy case to solve."

"That's why they sent us," said Springer. "The old firm, large as life and twice as natural. Join the C.I.D. and see the world, all expenses paid."

"We're here on duty, Jack, in case you've forgotten it," said Montero, who in fact enjoyed his sergeant's ebullience and allowed him a good deal of latitude. "We'd better go and look at that cabin again and see if we've missed anything. I'd ask Mr. Ludlow to come with us, but I'm sure he's in a hurry to get on shore and see the sights."

In spite of his fairly subtle character, Ludlow is one of the easiest men in the world to handle if one knows his weaknesses. The three of them walked out on deck, as the voice of Burrows intoned through the ship's loudspeakers that passengers must disembark at once for their shore excursion.

"I don't like to see them all going off like that, sir," Springer said. "One of them must be our man, and we've got them all cosily tucked up when they're on board. Suppose he does a bunk once he gets on shore?"

"We can't possibly stop them," Montero said. "You ought to know by now the restrictions which a democratic government places on its loyal coppers. But cheer up—their passports are all on board, so they've got to come back."

"Besides," Ludlow said, "these excursions are organized on the principle that tourists are stupid but potentially dangerous animals. Nobody has a chance of straying far from the main body, or the human sheep-dogs which accompany it."

They went down to the cabin, through a corridor that no longer throbbed with distant power. Everything looked neat and orderly, as if the ship was beginning a new voyage and the place was ready for occupation again. Only a slight crumpling of the cover on one bed remained as the token of sudden death. The tray and glass had been removed.

"We've sent everything to the police lab in Valetta," Montero explained. "They're going to rush through an analysis for us this morning, so we should be a bit further forward by the time we sail."

"I don't think much of these foreigners," Springer said. "They'll probably get it all mixed up."

"British subjects, Jack, or we wouldn't be having everything made so easy for us. And pretty efficient ones too from what we've seen of them. Now, Mr. Ludlow, I'll tell you what we've got so far. But you'll keep it to yourself, won't you?"

"I don't think you have found me unreliable in the past," Ludlow said huffily.

"No, we've had good reason to be grateful to you, even if you have sailed pretty close to the wind a few times. We seem to be full of nautical metaphors this morning. Anyway, we've had a good going-over for prints, and found quite a few. Some of them can probably be eliminated quickly—the dead woman, her cabin-companion, their stewardess and so on. There were no prints on the jug, but several on the tray. The glass had only one set—left-handed, and presumably those of Miss Acton herself."

Ludlow seemed not to be listening, but to be looking hard at the cabin telephone. However, it was neither fingerprints nor telephones that brought out his next question.

"Did you find any jewellery in the cabin?"

"How did you know about that?" Montero looked surprised for a moment. "I see you haven't been wasting your time. Yes, there was a box with a good deal of jewellery—pretty valuable stuff, as far as I could tell."

"It was lovely," Springer said. "The meanest fence in London would have given five thousand for it straight off."

"Springer's already working on the theory that theft was the motive. The snag is that the box was still here, and the stuff looked as if it had been carefully packed and not disturbed. Now, since most of the passengers are on shore, I think we'll ask a few questions among the crew. Then we can start on the passengers after lunch. We've checked through the passports, and they all seem to be in order. Perhaps we could find a cup of coffee, and get the general picture from you before we see anyone else."

They settled in the lounge, where Ludlow told them all he knew. He did it with what was, for him, a creditably small number of quotations and digressions. As the facts were brought out, and assembled methodically in Springer's notebook, it became obvious that a comparatively small number of people knew that the tray was intended for Diana Acton.

"That seems to be the main peg to hang things on for a start," Montero said. "Unless we've got a homicidal maniac on board, people don't go round dropping cyanide into orange juice at random. If we concentrate on motive and opportunity among those people who knew who had ordered that particular jug, we ought to get there. From what we've heard, the dead woman seems to have been a bit of a storm-centre. Is there anything else you can suggest, Mr. Ludlow?"

"I don't think so, except that you've just made another and perhaps unfortunate metaphor. In fact, the incidence of nautical expressions in our language is extremely interesting, though understandable when you consider our history. By the way, have you ever considered how the sailor in English fiction is almost invariably a noble and heroic character, whereas the soldier is more often than not a villain—at least until Kipling."

"That's true," Montero said with interest. "I suppose the fact that the professional army was used by the government as a police force—"

"If Mr. Ludlow can't tell us anything more, perhaps we ought to start questioning, sir," said Springer, who regarded his chief's literary interests as a burden to be borne and a dangerous interference with routine.

"What did you think of the cabin itself?" asked Ludlow, also recalled to the present.

"Nothing much there except for the prints and of course the jug and glass. The jewellery may or may not be important. There was no sign of any violence, or of the body having been moved," Montero said.

"No, I thought not. But there does seem to be something phoney about the whole thing."

"What exactly do you mean by that?"

"It's an American expression. I must have picked it up in talking to some of them," Ludlow said, as if it was a dangerous germ. "Though in this instance it might be reasonably appropriate. I'm going to sit in the sun."

He trotted off, and the two detectives went to the cabin which had been alloted to them. Relieved, perhaps, not to see a large band of London policemen in full uniform, the Captain had given orders that they were to be helped in every possible way. Burrows, with snobbishness suppressed by a desire to keep the company's name clean, was most attentive. When Montero said that they would like a word with Harmer first, the steward appeared with a speed that would have surprised the passengers whom he normally served. Montero went in without preliminaries.

"Did you prepare a tray for one of the cabins two nights ago?"

"I did, and it came at a very awkward time. Some passengers don't care how much extra work they give."

"Did you know that it was a tray for Miss Diana Acton?"

"Course I did. She's on one of my tables—that's why I was the one to get it ready."

"You regard Miss Acton as one of the more inconsiderate passengers? In fact, you disliked her?"

"You've no call to twist my words like that," Harmer said, looking almost as white as his uniform jacket. "I don't hold no opinions."

"Wise man. I wouldn't think of twisting anything. I was just offering sympathy."

Harmer looked unconvinced.

"What did you put on the tray?" Springer asked.

"Same as the Chief Steward said she'd asked for—bowl of fruit, plate and knife, jug of orange juice and a glass."

"What kind of fruit?"

"Blimey, I don't know. Orange, grapes, peach—they're all put out in individual bowls in the pantry, ready for the tables. I just took one."

"Where did the orange juice come from?"

"Out of the big glass container. There's always different juices, ready to serve."

"What about the jug and the glass?"

"I got them straight out of the clean store."

Montero, who had been nodding either with approval or drowsiness at his subordinate's questions, suddenly looked up with hardness in his blue eyes.

"You had a good opportunity of adding something to that orange juice, didn't you?"

"Not five minutes before dinner, with everybody going mad and the Chief Steward watching all you do. Anyway, where would I get cyanide from?"

"Who mentioned cyanide?"

The eyes were very cold now, but Harmer was unabashed.

"It's all over the ship. News travels fast at sea, you know. Everyone's heard that she was poisoned. But let me tell you, mister, it wasn't put in by me."

"All right, you can go now. Ask Mr. Burrows to come and see me."

Harmer found himself outside the cabin, with the mixture of relief and anxiety which Montero's calculated changes of tone generally produced in those he interrogated.

"Mr. Ludlow told us Harmer had admitted having words with Miss Acton. Why didn't you ask him about it, sir?" Springer asked a little reproachfully.

"Because he was expecting me to; it can wait. Not a very savoury character, but probably not a murderer, would you say?"

"Shouldn't wonder if he's got a record—small-time crook. He could have slipped the stuff in easy, in spite of what he says. But I don't think he's our man, somehow."

A polite knock on the door preceded Burrows, very neat and nervous. He was asked only to confirm that Julie West had changed cabins with Theresa, after Diana had made a fuss. He had seen a tray being taken down, and had been told that it was for Diana.

"Did you leave your desk between then and the discovery of the body?" Montero asked.

"Not for a moment. There was a good deal of paper work to be done, and I was going to have dinner later. My assistant can confirm that. I went to the cabin with Miss West and Mr. Ludlow—who, I understand, is a friend of yours, Inspector."

"I know him pretty well. What do you think of Harmer?"

"Harmer—the table-steward? Not very satisfactory, from what I've seen of him so far. Rather surly and unobliging. It's extremely difficult to get good men for that sort of work. But it isn't really my province. As Cruise Director I——"

"Yes, it doesn't matter. I'd like to see the stewardess who took down the tray."

Burrows also found himself outside in the corridor. His professional smile had disappeared and he looked nervous. His manner was lordly enough, however, when he sent for the stewardess and told her that the Inspector wanted to see her. She came, and stood in front of the table where Montero was sitting, her hands clasped in a respectful willingness to serve. Montero asked her to sit down, and looked at her for a few moments without speaking. She was a tall, dark woman of about thirty. Her face, heavy but not unattractive, showed nothing; and her neat uniform made her appear detached from the reality of daily bitterness that ended in death.

"What is your name?" Montero asked at last, quiet and polite.

"Nancy Benger."

"How long have you been a stewardess on this ship?"

"Since the beginning of the season. This is my fifth cruise in her."

"I see. Now, I understand that you looked after the cabin occupied by Miss Diana Acton and Miss—yes, Miss West."

"That's right. I look after all the ladies who have cabins in that corridor. There is a male steward as well."

"You took a tray to Miss Acton's cabin, on the evening before last. Will you please tell me exactly what you did, from the time of being told to do so."

"The Chief Steward rang to the stewards' pantry on my deck and said that Miss Acton was having a tray instead of dinner. As she was in one of my cabins, it was my job to collect the tray and take it down. I went up to the dining-saloon pantry, and the tray was waiting for me. I took it and——"

"I'm sorry to interrupt you, but what exactly do you mean that the tray was waiting for you?"

"It was prepared and left on one of the tables. The Chief Steward showed me where it was."

"Who had prepared it?"

"It would be Miss Acton's table-steward. I've no idea who that is."

"What was on the tray?"

"It was covered with a cloth. I didn't look."

"So you took it out of the pantry. What then?"

"I went down as far as the main foyer, where I had to

cross over for the stairs to the next deck. Mr. Burrows called me over and asked to see the tray."

"Would he usually do that?" Springer asked, looking up from his notebook like an eager bloodhound.

"I've never known him to do it before. And he hasn't got any right to interfere either. I answer to the Head Cabin Steward, and then to the Purser. Mr. Burrows is to look after the cruise arrangements, and not to start interfering with the ordinary running of the ship——"

"But you obeyed him this time?" Montero asked, hastily cutting off the flow of indignation.

"There was no point in making an issue of it. I didn't want to start a row, not with the passengers standing there."

"What passengers?" Montero and Springer asked together like the well-trained chorus of a comic opera.

"They were standing by the desk, cashing cheques, I think. It was Mrs. Grossheim and Mr. Mallaby—they're both in cabins in my section."

"What did Mr. Burrows do when you took over the tray?"

"I put it down on his desk. He picked it up and took it to the back, where he seemed to have a good look at it."

"Could you see his movements all the time?"

"He had his back to me. I could see that he lifted the cloth, but that's all. Then he brought the tray back, asked if Miss Acton was ill, and told me to be sure to give the tray to her personally. I said that I was to leave it outside the door, and he said nothing, and I took it and I did."

"I'd just like to get that straight," said Springer, troubled by the abrupt and involved ending of the story. "You put the tray down outside the cabin door?"

"That's right. The message from the Chief Steward had said to leave it outside the door."

"Didn't it seem a bit funny to you that it wasn't to be taken in—or indeed that a tray was asked for at all?"

"No." Nancy looked surprised. "Why, bless you, the ladies are always asking for trays of fruit and soft drinks, especially in the hot weather. They're so worried about their figures that they waste half the good food they could have. As for leaving it outside the door, they often ask for that if they're going to change or have a shower or something. I'd done exactly the same for Miss Acton two nights before. She didn't eat enough, if you ask me, and what good has it done her now? Thank God I don't have to worry."

She smoothed her white uniform complacently over her slender stomach.

"Was the cabin door locked?" Montero asked.

"I don't know; I didn't try. I just put down the tray, and knocked and said, 'Your tray, Miss Acton,' and went. I didn't expect an answer."

"What did you do then?"

"Went and had my supper. Oh, Mr. Acton and his wife were just coming out of their cabin. He asked me who the tray was for, and I told him."

"Were any of the other cabin doors open?"

"I couldn't say."

"Just one more question, Miss Benger. Have you, at any time on this trip, seen a tin marked 'Cyanide' in any of the cabins under your care?"

"I've seen no such thing. And I don't go poking into cupboards either. I can tell you, there are some stewardesses on this ship who'd——"

"All right, thank you very much. You've been most helpful."

Mollified, Nancy Benger went out. Montero and Springer looked at each other with expressions that many London criminals would have recognized and known to forebode no good.

"That was a bit of a surprise packet, sir," Springer said. "With what Mr. Ludlow's told us already, it looks as if a hell of a lot of people knew about that tray and who it was for. Are you going to have Burrows down again?"

"Later, Jack. The longer he thinks we don't know about that little episode, the more he's likely to give himself away. If there's anything to give, because frankly I can't see any reason why he should take such a risk so openly. I don't like this sort of case—it's too easy in some ways and damned difficult in others. Plenty of people could have poisoned that orange juice, but there's no clear pointer to any of them. Not yet, anyway, but we've still got the reports to come from the lab in Valetta. When we've talked to some of the passengers, we can start to make a sensible analysis. I think we've about exhausted this morning's possibilities. The doctor didn't give us much help, did he?"

"I don't think he liked being got out of bed so early," Springer said with a grin.

"Well, we had to make a start somewhere, and it would take a braver man than me to face Ludlow's flow of invective at that hour. No, the doctor doesn't seem very helpful, but at least he did remove and preserve the contents of the stomach. I wish he could have been more precise about the time of death, though the limits are pretty well fixed by evidence of witnesses. See if you can get hold of the Chief Steward."

"I'll go and find out what's for lunch, sir," Springer said.

The scene in the pantry was a few degrees less feverish before lunch than before dinner. However, the Chief Steward was reluctant to come and leave things unattended; but Springer had a technique for persuading reluctant witnesses, without breaking any rules. As they made their way down the passengers were returning from the morning's excursion. Already signs of departure were evident, for the *Inquirer* was to sail for Naples shortly after noon.

The Chief Steward confirmed what Harmer and Nancy had already said. He himself had taken the telephone call from Miss Acton's cabin.

"Are you sure that it was Miss Acton? Did you recognize her voice?" Montero asked.

"Well—she said she was. I mean, I can't swear to it, can I? I don't know that I ever had occasion to speak to her personally. But I knew her by sight of course. It was the sort of voice I should have expected her to have, if you take my meaning."

"Nothing distinctive about it? No special accent, or impediment or anything like that?"

"Just a nice English lady's voice. She was very nice—said she was sorry to give us the trouble at such short notice. But of course I told her it was no trouble at all. Lots of the ladies have trays sent down, especially in the hot weather."

"So I believe. I expect you want to get back to your duties now."

The Chief Steward went, like a man who has the sole responsibility for a great and crucial battle. Montero stretched wearily and looked at his subordinate.

"Time to break for lunch," he said.

"I should think so, sir," Springer replied. "All this talk about trays of fruit makes me feel starving. Those women must all be daft."

— 9 —

Nobody ever knew what vexing calculations of protocol it had cost the Purser, in consultation with Burrows, but Montero and Springer were given a table in the first-class saloon. It was not an honourable table, being far from the service and crowded against a pillar, but their appetites did not seem to suffer. On deck after lunch they joined Ludlow, who was leaning on the rail and watching Malta slip away into the distance.

"Did you have a good morning?" he asked them.

"An interesting one at least," Montero said, "and this afternoon promises to be even more interesting."

"Can I come and listen?" Ludlow asked, with a child-like eagerness that made Montero quickly hide a smile.

"Now, Mr. Ludlow, you know very well that I can't let you be present during an official investigation. If I choose to talk things over with you later, that's another matter."

"Don't tell me anything you don't want to," Ludlow said loftily.

"And don't you try to be cool with me, because you'll be bursting to hear it, and I've got good reason to value your judgement. So that's settled, and you can have a nice afternoon looking at the sea, while we work in a stuffy cabin."

"I've come to the conclusion that looking at the sea is an occupation that's soon exhausted," Ludlow said. "Johnson remarked that one green field was much like another. One piece of sea is even more like another. Like

Johnson, I am beginning to prefer the idea of a walk down Fleet Street."

"He also said," Montero reminded him, "that being in a ship is like being in prison, with the additional danger of being drowned. So there's a thought to keep you company."

Ludlow sighed, perhaps from boredom with the sea, perhaps because he seldom got the better of Montero in quotation. Springer looked pensive as he followed his chief.

"What you said about being in prision, it's true isn't it? I mean, here we've got all our suspects in one place and none of them can get away. We don't have any trouble about holding them, and they can't start shouting for a solicitor."

"But don't forget that in a few days they'll all disperse like a lot of rabbits and we may have the devil of a job to get them in one place again, so we've got to work fast. Find David Acton and bring him along."

David Acton came unwillingly, with a scowl that made him look unprepossessing in spite of his neat appearance and his pleasantly sunburnt features. He glared at Montero, dropped heavily into a chair and waited. Montero took his time putting some papers into a neat pile before saying, quietly and conversationally:

"I believe that you will profit financially from your sister's death, Mr. Acton."

"Who told you that?" David was clearly taken aback and alarmed.

"Is it not true then?"

"It's true that I'm her heir. All right—she had most of the family money, I've hardly been able to keep the business going without any capital, and I've had to borrow from her. So you've convinced yourself that I killed her. Now go ahead and prove it."

Montero appeared not to have heard any of this.

"Why did you leave the saloon during dinner, on the

evening that your sister was killed?" he asked, still quietly.

"You don't know that she was killed. It could have been suicide."

"We are treating this case as one of murder. Will you answer my question, please?"

"I don't have to tell you anything."

"That is perfectly true. Even innocent persons sometimes refuse to answer questions—but not very often."

"Look here, Inspector or whatever you call yourself, this is intolerable. You're practically accusing me of killing my sister—my own sister. But you're not dealing with an uneducated criminal now. You're not going to trap me into anything. I shall get protection—I'll—I'll make a complaint about you."

"That is your privilege, sir."

There was a long silence. Montero and Springer seemed to be concerned with their notes. David Acton half rose, then sat down again and twisted about uncomfortably.

"I went to get something from my cabin," he said at last.

"To get what?" Montero asked, as if the previous outburst had never happened.

"Oh—a clean handkerchief. I'd spilled something on myself—I mean, I wanted to use warm water—and the cabin——" His voice trailed off.

"Quite so, Mr. Acton," Montero said encouragingly. "So you went to your cabin. Not to your sister's cabin?"

"No! I mean, of course, it was next to ours."

"So I have learnt. You must have noticed whether the tray was still outside."

"It wasn't there. I saw the stewardess putting it down, when my wife and I were going up to dinner. It wasn't there later."

"Was your sister left-handed?"

"Yes, she was. But why——"

"Would she be likely to pour out a drink and swallow

it quickly, without fussing whether it was all right?"

"Yes, that's exactly what she was like. We used to tease her sometimes about being a quick drinker. She was very impetuous—about some things, that is."

"But not about others, such as money matters?"

"You're trying to trap me again, about money. I tell you I'm not an ignorant man that you can do as you like with——" This time David was fully on his feet.

"I do not underestimate your intelligence, sir. It makes your unwillingness to answer questions more significant. I should like to speak to your daughter, if she can spare me a few minutes."

"Don't talk to Theresa. She's quite irresponsible. You can't believe a word she says."

"Let me be judge of that, please."

"I just can't remember what can happen to you for hitting a witness, but I think it might be worth it," Springer said after David had muttered himself out of the cabin.

"I'd rather keep him intact for the time being. There's something to be said for getting over the worst at the beginning of the afternoon."

Montero was too optimistic, for when Theresa arrived it was obvious that she was in one of her moods. She was wearing a two-piece bathing-suit, and the robe which she had pulled on was deliberately allowed to fall open around her when she sat down, Springer modestly averted his eyes.

"I'm sorry to interrupt your sun-bathing, Miss Acton," Montero said. "I hope you've been enjoying your holiday, though your aunt's death must have been a terrible shock for you. Do you find that a cruise is a pleasant way of seeing new places?"

"You'rc trying to put me at my ease, aren't you? You needn't bother—I'm not in the least afraid of you."

"I'm very glad to hear it, because I should hate to frighten anyone so charming."

"You won't get me that way either. I know all about men. You sit there pretending to be official, and all the time you're thinking how you'd like to seduce me."

Springer gulped and slip lower in his chair.

"I haven't the least desire to seduce you, Miss Acton."

"Why, are you queer?" Theresa asked with interest.

Springer nearly disappeared under the table.

"It just happens that I don't try to seduce schoolgirls. Could you manage to answer a few questions, or do you want to go back on deck?"

"What do you want to know?" Theresa scowled, drew the robe around her and looked a little less confident.

"First, why you changed your cabin after the first night."

"I couldn't get on with Diana. Nobody could. It wasn't anything really, but we just kept quarrelling about where to put things, and having the light on and that sort of thing. She always threw her weight about because she had all the money. So don't expect me to say that I'm sorry she's dead. Now I've shocked you."

"Don't waste your time trying to shock me, because nothing does. In any case, you were not the only one to quarrel with Miss Acton. There was Mr. Penge, for example."

"Rupert? He didn't do it. They only say that because they're jealous of us. Diana tried to turn them against him. She didn't want him herself, and she wouldn't let anyone else have him. She was horrid to him that day on Rhodes when he was just trying to be polite—but he didn't do it."

She put her hand to her mouth and looked so much like a frightened schoolgirl that Springer cautiously raised himself an inch or two in his chair.

"If Mr. Penge didn't do it, who did?" Montero asked calmly.

"That man Burrows. He didn't want to change the cabin and she said she'd report him. And then when he came into my cabin, Diana saw him and said she'd report him for that too."

"But what was Burrows doing in your cabin?"

"It was just after we'd changed over. He came in to see

if I was all right and had everything—so he said. Of course, he wanted to seduce me, but he didn't try anything. Then Diana came to bring some things I'd left, and she said he had no right to be in a passenger's cabin and she'd report him. I'm sure he did it."

"I see. Thank you for the tip," Montero said gravely. "Did you by any chance give him some of your cyanide for the purpose?"

"You know about that?"

"We know about most things. It was really very naughty of you to carry it about with you."

"I didn't carry it about, I kept it in the cabin, in the bathroom cabinet. And I bought it openly in London, and signed for it, so I did nothing wrong. You'd do anything to get me into your clutches, wouldn't you?"

"You took the tin with you when you changed cabins?"

"Yes. And I threw it overboard, the night after we left Athens. There's none in the cabin now. Ask Mrs. Pig, if you don't believe me."

"Who's Mrs. Pig?"

"The French woman who shares my cabin. I can't remember her name, but I call her that because she's so fat. She snores too."

"You are unlucky in your choice of companions. Would you ask your mother to come and see me? And please don't take poison about with you again. It may give you a sense of importance, but I hope you've seen what trouble it can cause."

Chastened but defiant, Theresa flounced to the door, looked with scorn at both the men and went out. Springer, red in the face, muttered, "Stone the crows," and looked as if he wanted fresh air. Montero, however, was happy.

"Very interesting," he said. "Burrows could have got hold of some cyanide while he was prowling around her cabin that second night. And we know, though she doesn't, of the opportunity he had to use it."

"Not much of a motive though, sir."

"No, but still—on the other hand that girl may be covering up for her father, who's obviously got something to hide."

After the rest of the family, Elizabeth seemed refreshingly normal. She told her story as she had told it to Ludlow on the previous day, and confirmed that David had gone down to clean his suit after spilling something at dinner. She was reserved on the subject of Rupert Penge but could find nothing really to say against him.

Julie West came next, and once again they learned little to supplement the account which had already come to them by way of Ludlow.

"When you went back to the cabin after dinner, the door was unlocked as you'd left it?" Montero asked eventually.

"Sure, I just turned the handle and went in, and—oh!"

"I don't like recalling that dreadful experience to you, Miss West, but did anything strike you about the cabin—anything at all that was different from when you went out?"

"I don't think so. I just didn't stop to look, as soon as I saw Diana on the bed. The tray was there, right beside her. I didn't notice anything else."

"I have formed the impression that a number of people on board disliked Miss Acton. Did you know of any particular enemies she may have had?"

"Why, no. I don't think she had any enemies. She sure made some people get a bit mad at her, but she was a fine girl really. No one could want to kill her."

"Apparently someone did. About these investments that she was thinking of making in your property: did either of you discuss them with anyone else?"

"I didn't, until I told Professor Ludlow yesterday. I don't know if she did. Anyway, she hadn't decided, it was just an idea she was thinking over."

"Thank you, Miss West. Do tell us at once if anything occurs to you that could have even the slightest bearing on all this."

"Just one thing," said Springer, who had at last recovered from Theresa, "you're sure she didn't eat or drink anything between lunch and dinner on the day she died?"

"Well, we met up on deck about half two, like I told Professor Ludlow. She didn't have anything there—wouldn't even join me when I went for some juice. We had sherry in the cabin—and that was the last time I saw her alive."

"She hadn't rung for the tray before you left?"

"Well, no, but she was just picking up the phone."

"I had a word with the steward who runs the bar on the sun-deck," Springer said when Julie had gone, "and he remembers her coming up for one drink. The other girl didn't have anything. We're going to look a bit silly if there was nothing in that jug of orange juice."

"There has to be. It doesn't matter whether or not she had anything before, because cyanide's one of the quickest killers there is. Now stretch those long legs of yours, and find Rupert Penge. He'll probably be sun-bathing with Theresa Acton."

"I don't fancy seeing her again. I've seen her sort when I was on the beat. Always bringing charges against some poor bloke who only looked at them. I don't know what the wife would say if she knew——"

Springer went out grumbling, and soon returned with Rupert Penge, who was looking as condescending as he could in shorts and bright shirt. Montero, having coped with young barristers while Rupert was at school, soon got the questioning going as he wanted it. It was established that Diana had sharply and indeed rudely rebuffed Rupert when he had tried to get friendly with her.

"Miss Acton was a very attractive woman, I believe," Montero said.

"In her way. She wasn't my type really. I only made up to her so that I could get on with Theresa, which I've done. She's a real honey."

"Yes, Sergeant Springer and I have had the opportunity of—er—of observing her. Did Miss Diana Acton encourage your new friendship?"

"She tried to break it up, but that was the surest way of getting Theresa closer to me. I never cared anything for Diana."

"Or for her considerable fortune?"

"That sort of question could get you into serious trouble, Inspector."

"I don't see why, sir. I merely remarked that you cared nothing for her fortune. Which now goes to her brother, and no doubt eventually to your friend her niece. Do you want to dispute any of that? No? Then we needn't keep you any longer."

Springer was now bursting with theories, but Montero sent him to fetch Adrian Mallaby, who came in bold and confident. He cheerfully admitted overhearing the conversation with Burrows about the tray. He had just come up from his cabin, leaving Rupert Penge down there still dressing. After changing some money, he had gone straight up to dinner.

"One of the first in," he recalled. "Even beat your pal the Professor, and his American girl-friend. That chap Ludlow, he isn't all he seems, is he?"

"Few of us are, Mr. Mallaby. Why did you leave dinner early?"

"I'd finished—started early, finished early. Too hot in there, after a day in the sun. I didn't want to sit yarning with the American girl and the two old dears at my table. It's a free ocean, as the saying goes."

"What did you do when you left the dining-saloon?"

"Walked round the deck a few times."

"You didn't go to your cabin?"

"I did not."

"Did you have any reason to dislike Miss Acton?"

"Dislike her? We got on splendidly and she seemed to take to me. One in the eye for the young ones, what? We older chaps can show them a thing or two. I bet you've got a pretty crafty line in chat yourself under that official moustache of yours. I tell you what, old boy, I wish I could help you to find who killed her, I really do. She was a great little kid."

"I see what you mean about hitting witnesses, Jack," Montero said when Mallaby had gone. "Go and get Mrs. Grossheim, and we'll see if we can get a different opinion on Diana."

They got it, caustically and at length. Cornelia Grossheim was of the opinion that Diana had been a homebreaker, a siren, a brightly scarlet woman. She had even made the ever-virtuous Joseph P. Grossheim stray from his conjugal path.

"I was sorry for that nice girl Julie West going in with her, I really was," Cornelia said. "That young niece who went out is no better than her, if you ask my opinion. I think it's just terrible how these young girls——"

"Did you tell your husband that a tray was being taken down for Miss Acton?" Montero almost shouted in desperation.

"I sure did. After I had heard the girl tell Mr. Burrows, I went straight down and there was the tray outside the door. I told Joseph that she was staying in her cabin, and I told him to get right upstairs to dinner and not have any ideas about it."

"But you didn't go to dinner yourself?"

"I didn't want to eat a thing. I had a headache, what with the sun and the fuss about Joseph, and all these different currencies—when dollars and cents are so easy to handle any place—that I just lay down and went to sleep. I didn't want a tray, I didn't want anything but a couple of tranquillizers."

"When did you wake up?"

"When I heard all that screaming and shouting outside in the corridor. I went out and there was Julie and that Mr. Ludlow, and I looked in and saw the Acton woman lying there dead. It was just awful."

"So you didn't hear any movement in the corridor during dinner."

"I slept the whole time. I wouldn't have wakened but

for all the noise. Those tranquillizers are fine. My physician back home told me——"

"Please ask your husband to be so kind as to come and see me," said Montero, a hunted look in his usually calm face.

Joseph Grossheim repeated what he had told Ludlow, omitting the preliminary fiction about his unfortunate friend. He looked terrified all through the interview, but whether from awe of English policemen or of his wife it was impossible to say. Cornelia had told him that the tray, which he had noticed outside the cabin, was for Diana.

"Then why did you give Mr. Ludlow the impression that you didn't know who the tray was for?" Montero asked.

"Well—I guess I was just making conversation. Maybe I didn't want to show too much interest in Diana. I don't know."

Joseph was allowed to go, which he did thankfully. Montero looked at the amassed paper on the table and sighed.

"I think we'll take this lot out in the sun. But first, find out what Theresa's Mrs. Pig is really called, and see if you can get her to come."

Mrs. Pig was in fact Madame Mercier, a widow from Orléans, whom Ludlow would have recognized as the very fat woman who had pushed him aside when they were disembarking at Rhodes. Her English, however, was thin; and Montero's French was even thinner. He persevered, and learned that she had a poor opinion of Theresa.

"*Une gamine, celle-ci.* Makes to excite the boys but not to give the love, eh? *Moi, je connais bien le grand amour. Parfois, quand mon pauvre mari——*"

"*Oui. Naturellement.* Now, did you ever see any cyanide in your cabin after Miss Acton moved in?"

"*Comment?*"

"*Avez-vous vu du—damn—Mademoiselle Therese Acton, a-t-elle possedé du—de la—du poison?*"

"Je ne sais pas, monsieur. Cela ne me ferait rien."

Did you ever see a tin—*une boîte de fer blanc*—hidden away—er—*cache?*"

Madame Mercier explained at length that she did not occupy herself with what others had hidden away. She had seen no such tin, and she was not in the habit of looking in cupboards——

"Thank you very much—*merci beaucoup, madame. Très* helpful—very *gentille—merci beaucoup.*"

"Je vous en prie, monsieur. Au revoir."

Montero wiped his face.

"That was smashing, sir," Springer said admiringly. "Where did you learn to parlee-voo like that?"

"There ought to be a rude answer, but I can't think of it. Let's get out of here."

— 10 —

The passengers on the *Inquirer* had got used to Ludlow's tweed suit, but when he was joined by two companions who seemed equally unprepared for hot weather there was a good deal of interest from the brown devotees of the sun-deck. It was soon known that the two new arrivals were detectives and this caused some reappraisal of Ludlow's position. Some held that he was a detective disguised as a university lecturer, who had been expecting the murder of Diana Acton and unable to prevent it. Others argued that he must be a scientist, called in to assist Scotland Yard on some technical points. While a new character was thus being built up for him, Ludlow sat in a quiet corner with Montero and Springer. Malta was already out of sight and blue water once more stretched in every direction. Springer, his coat removed to display startling crimson braces, was discoursing happily on the pleasures of cruising when the Inspector recalled him to duty.

"We'd better go through everybody and see what we've got," said Montero. "I've no doubt that she made a good many enemies, though that's probably true for all of us. She was poisoned by cyanide in the orange juice—but we'll come to the analyst's report later. There was a tin of cyanide standing blatantly in that girl's cabin for several days; anyway, her possession of it shows that the stuff is scandalously easy to get hold of. The jug of orange juice was left outside in the corridor where anyone could have got at it."

"Anyone on the ship could have done it," Springer remarked sadly.

"In theory, yes. But I'm going to concentrate on the members of the crew who handled the tray and the passengers who were in cabins near to Diana Acton's. They all seem to have been mixed up with her in some way. Right, Jack, let's look for motive and opportunity, since the means are clear enough."

"I've sorted them out into what Mr. Ludlow would call a logical order. The first to be near the tray was Harmer, the steward who made it up. He knew who it was for, and he had plenty of chance to slip some poison into the jug. He admits that things are confused in the pantry just before dinner, and he can't possibly have been watched all the time. He'd had words with the murdered woman, though that doesn't seem much of a motive to me. Even if she got him sacked, which is unlikely, he's obviously the sort who drifts from one job to another——"

"All right, spare us the benefits of psychology. Somebody had a good enough motive to do it. I agree that I'd like a stronger one than Harmer seems to have had. Who next?"

"Nancy Benger, the stewardess. She could easily have poisoned the drink on her way down, since she'd have been out of view when she was on one of the stairways. The trouble is, she doesn't seem to have any motive at all. Now, Miss Acton was rich and had some very valuable jewellery in her cabin. Suppose this stewardess had pinched some, and she'd found out and was threatening to—what do you think, Mr. Ludlow?" Springer appealed for support as he saw his superior's eye turning coldly on his speculations.

"I think that the presence of that jewellery in the cabin is very significant," Ludlow said, "but I shouldn't like to develop that just at present. It may be that academic caution can be overdone, to the extent of seeking never to be committed on anything, but there is in fact a great virtue in not taking one fact in isolation. I remember once in my research coming upon what seemed to be unmistakable evidence of——"

"On the way down, she was stopped by Burrows," Montero said desperately as the whole investigation seemed likely to slip away over the side. "He took the tray, examined it with his back turned and could very easily have used poison. He knew it was for Miss Acton, with whom he'd had a row about changing her cabin; and young Theresa tells us that she'd told him off for being where he shouldn't."

"I didn't know all that about Burrows," Ludlow said. "I wondered why he started becoming so unwontedly civil yesterday."

"Thank goodness there's something you don't claim to know, Mr. Ludlow—it makes a change. Now come to the passengers," Montero added hastily before Ludlow could start again.

"David Acton, the murdered woman's brother, who inherits her money and seems to have been in need of it too. He saw the tray delivered and he left the dining-saloon during dinner on what I for one don't reckon to be a very good excuse. He looks to me like the one to watch, sir."

"I think I agree, so far. But what about his wife? She stood to gain as much by getting money into the family business, and she wouldn't have any fraternal feelings for the girl."

"But when could she have done it?" Springer asked. "Unless she did it with her husband looking on and encouraging her before they went up to dinner. Because she didn't go out again."

"That's true. What about the daughter, Theresa?"

"Ah, what indeed, sir. I can't remember any girls like that when I was young. I mean, we used to like a bit of fun and we never reckoned to be specially high-class in what we said. But there wasn't a kid in the whole of Bermondsey who'd have talked to a couple of grown men like she did."

"It's nothing to be alarmed about," Ludlow said. "The very young always choose a new way of shocking their elders in every generation. Not so long ago it would have been the affectation of religious scepticism. Now they like to pretend——"

"Oh shut up, you two. You ought to be an academic, Jack—and I don't mean that as a compliment. You're the most digressive policeman I've ever had the misfortune to work with. Get back to the point." Montero glared at his companions, and Springer went back hastily to his notebook.

"Theresa Acton. Niece of the deceased. Seemed to have a general dislike of her, with a special row about the cabin they shared. She also resented the money not belonging to her parents. She possessed a large amount of cyanide. She was told, by her mother, about the presence of the tray and who it was for. She seems to have hung about and come up to dinner late, so she had a good opportunity to do it."

"That's better. Stick to the point, and we may be able to call you a detective one day. Add that Theresa is obviously keen on Rupert Penge, and that she was trying to throw suspicion on Burrows. We only have her word for the row over Burrows in her cabin. Now Penge has got himself mixed up with the Acton family. Apparently Diana had put him in his place and he then played up to Theresa, with more success. So if he's hoping to marry her, he'd be interested in getting Diana's money diverted to that side of the family. What else have we got on him?"

"If everybody's told the truth, he was in his cabin, with the door partly open, when the tray was brought and questions asked about it. We don't know what chance he had to do anything, though."

"We do," said Ludlow, who had been neglected long enough. "He came rather late to dinner that night—after Theresa Acton. He sits at my table."

"So he had plenty of time. What do you think of him?" Montero asked.

"I dislike him, but that doesn't make him a murderer. He is certainly ambitious and acquisitive. He is also intolerably facetious and argumentative."

"I see. Was it unusual for him to be late for a meal?"

"No. That's another thing I dislike about him. He wanders in whenever he feels like it, making some inane remark to those of us who contrived to be there at the right time. It's just as easy to be punctual——"

"Yes, yes. What was his manner like on that night?"

"Quieter than usual. I thought he seemed worried. Perhaps it was just hunger, because he became repulsively normal later."

"He and the girl could have done it between them," Springer said. "She gave him the poison and egged him on, then went away while he did it."

"Perhaps. He was taking a lot on trust, if that was his way of getting rich. Who else?"

"Julie West, the American girl who shared Miss Acton's cabin. She's an important witness, since she was the last to see Miss Acton alive. She joined you on deck at what time, Mr. Ludlow?"

"About ten minutes before dinner, I think. She sat and talked, rather boringly, until we went in to dinner and separated."

"Did she leave before the end?"

"No—at the same time as I did. Then she ran back and told me what she had found."

"So she couldn't have done anything with the tray, which wasn't ordered or delivered to the cabin until she was already on deck with you," Montero said.

"But what about when she went down and discovered the body?" asked Springer.

Ludlow shook his head. "She was back almost at once," he said. "No time to poison the jug, take it in and get Diana to drink it."

"Besides, the doctor was sure that she had been dead at least half an hour when he examined her," Montero said. "Not that he seems to know much of his own business, but he'd certainly know if she'd died only a few minutes before. Anyway, the two seem to have got on quite well—Julie and Diana, I mean. They'd just spent the afternoon together, amicably enough. Nobody can be eliminated yet, but I don't intend to waste much time on Miss West. Then there were the two Americans."

"The lady, Mrs. Grossheim, was standing at the desk when Burrows looked at the tray," Springer said. "She then went down, and stayed in her cabin all through dinner. She could have slipped out and done it any time. On the other hand, she may have told her husband, and he had time to do it—was he late to dinner that night, Mr. Ludlow?"

"Yes, he was. I sat alone at my table, which the Grossheims also share, for a long time."

"Motive?" Montero asked.

"Only that the old man had made a pretty unsuccessful pass at Miss Acton, and his wife knew about it. Not very good. Then there was Adrian Mallaby—you know, sir, I'm sure I've seen him somewhere before."

"In what circumstances?"

"Ah, that's just it. Giving evidence, maybe. I can't remember. Anyway, he was at the desk too, and heard all about the tray. He came out of dinner before the end, says he stayed on deck but has no witnesses to prove it. If David Acton is telling the truth about the tray being gone when he went down during dinner, that lets out Mallaby completely. Also Julie West, of course. Mallaby doesn't seem to have had any motive at all."

"No," Montero agreed. "He seems to have been getting on very well with Diana, to the chagrin of Rupert Penge. In fact the two men openly quarrelled. Well, there it is. What do you think of it?"

Ludlow had apparently gone to sleep in the hot sun, but he soon became alert when asked for his opinion.

"The most obvious thing is the absence of any really strong motives outside the immediate family—as far as we know," he said. "So we must be prepared to dig deeper.

I'll do what I can in that way. But I'm still waiting for the wonders of science to be opened to me."

"The various analyses were made this morning," said Montero, who knew Ludlow well enough to interpret him. "The police lab in Valetta was extremely efficient and got the reports to us before we sailed. There's no doubt at all that she died of cyanide poisoning, which of course takes effect almost immediately. She had nothing in her stomach but about a glassful of orange juice and a little alcoholic liquid, probably sherry—and poison, of course. That ties in with what Miss West told us; the deck steward confirms that Miss Acton ordered nothing to eat or drink the whole afternoon, and didn't leave the deck. The orange juice left in the jug contained a large dose of cyanide—one glass of it would have killed ten people. The drop of sherry in the two glasses was all right, so was the bottle of sherry. The fruit on the tray was clear too. Now you've got the report on dabs, Jack."

"Miss Acton's prints, left hand, were on the glass. There were no prints on the jug. The tray was clean too, except for one lovely print of a full right hand, underneath. There were a few in the cabin, some of them Miss Acton's. The place was kept pretty clean. The door-handle was too smeared to give anything useful, but on the door itself there was a full left-hand print—not Miss Acton's."

"Right. Now go to the radio-office. Tell the A.C. by cable that we're on board and proceeding with routine investigations. The old man is a bit het-up about this case, because it's on a British ship sailing from a foreign port, with quite a few foreign passengers on board. Could be tricky. And get the other information we want."

Springer uncoiled himself regretfully from his deckchair and went. Montero and Ludlow sat and looked at the sea, and spoke a little of life and of death. Springer was soon back, looking pleased with himself.

"I sent the cable, sir," he said. "And I've checked on any messages that Miss Acton sent or received, like you told me."

"Well?" Montero asked hastily, before Ludlow could start a lecture on grammar.

"She made a call to London by radio-telephone. I've got the number. That was on the day before she was killed, in the morning. She received a call late that same afternoon. There were no other calls or cables."

"All right. I'll check on what those calls were about. You get round and collect prints from all the people on our list. Persuade them it's for elimination purposes—which it largely is. And remember you can't force any of them, or threaten them if they refuse."

"I know, sir," Springer said, sadly and with dignity. "A copper's life is very hard, with all the restrictions."

"It must have been experience of men like you that made the British resist the formation of a police force for so many years. Go and see what you can find."

"I think I'll go and see what I can find too," Ludlow said.

— 11 —

"I don't think much of this tea, sir," Sergeant Springer declared an hour later. "The lads at my first station could have shown them how to brew a decent cup."

He was sitting with Montero in a corner of the first-class lounge, drinking china tea and sorting out a number of small cards. He looked very pleased with life, in spite of his strictures on the refreshment.

"They all co-operated," he said, "all except that fellow Mallaby. I wish I could remember where I've seen him before—I bet he's got a record, and that's why he wouldn't give his dabs. Some of them made a bit of fuss, but I just persuaded them gently, like you said."

"I'm sure you were the soul of courtesy, but don't expect me to speak up for you when they all write to their M.P.s as soon as they get home. Now tell me what you've learned that's making you look like a hungry but contented cat."

"The cabin didn't give us much. There were traces from the two ladies who occupied it, and from the stewardess. As we said before, it was pretty clean anyway. But here's the pay-off. That print on the door was from David Acton's left hand, the print under the tray was from his right hand. What do you say now, sir?"

"Nothing, except that you've done a good job. I'm not going to run and arrest Acton immediately, but I certainly want to have another talk with him. It's the negative results that worry me most at present."

Springer looked puzzled. "I don't follow you, sir," he said.

"Why were there no prints on the jug, and none on the tray except for that one underneath? Even if the murderer wore gloves, we ought to have found prints from Harmer, the stewardess, Burrows and Miss Acton herself. It's obvious that the tray and the jug were wiped, but the print underneath the tray was missed. That doesn't let out David Acton, because he must have touched the edge of the tray before he got his hand underneath, unless he's a juggler."

Springer sat and shuffled his little cards. Montero drank some more tea and elegantly nibbled a small biscuit. The noises from the sun-deck floated through the open windows of the lounge.

"Try this one for size, sir," Springer said at last. "Acton put poison in the jug before going up to dinner, and carried it into the cabin. He wanted to make sure that nobody else got hold of it. Then he went back during dinner, to see that she'd drunk the stuff and to wipe off the prints. Only he forgot how he'd held the tray, and missed the big one."

"A bit messy, Jack. Why did he ever hold the tray in that awkward way—and why was his other hand on the door? Still, you've made a point. If the stuff was poisoned and then left outside the door, the murderer took the risk of someone else picking it up and perhaps drinking it. He must have been either very callous or very unimaginative. More likely that he waited until the tray was taken in by Miss Acton herself, before leaving. That could account for most of those in the adjacent cabins. Or there may have been two in it—one poisoned the stuff and the other stayed behind to wipe off the prints. But anybody so aware of the danger would surely have worn thin gloves. By the way, there wasn't anything on the jewel box, was there?"

"Only from Burrows and Miss Acton. But that's another thing—what did she want to get those jewels out for? Do you think she was being blackmailed and was going to use them to pay somebody off?"

"It's possible, but it makes the mystery worse because

it's usually the blackmailer and not his victim who gets murdered."

Before Springer could make any reply, a large figure loomed over the table. Ludlow had appeared, almost dragging a red-faced and anxious Julie West.

"Sit down," said Ludlow, pointing to an empty chair and looking like a man receiving candidates for a difficult oral examination. Julie West subsided.

"Miss West has something to tell you," he went on.

"Yes?" said Montero encouragingly, while Springer fished out his notebook.

"I guess it's nothing, Inspector. I don't want to waste your time, and maybe you'll just laugh at me. I did think I ought to tell you this morning, but it seemed so silly. Then he came again, and I told Professor Ludlow, and he said I must come and tell you."

"Get your facts in order," Ludlow said firmly but kindly. "Always introduce your subject by a general declaration of purpose, then let the argument develop in logical sequence. The subject is Adrian Mallaby. Go on from there."

"Yeah. Thank you. Well, Inspector, maybe you know that Diana and Adrian Mallaby had been seeing a good bit of each other, the last day or two before she was killed. Well, on the night before, after the dance, she told me that she was frightened of him, that he was threatening her in some way. I said, why did she go on seeing him and dancing with him? She said she had to, but she wouldn't say why. I told her, if anything was wrong, she ought to go and see Mr. Burrows, or maybe the Captain. I don't think she did, though."

"Did she give you no idea of why she was frightened?" Montero said.

"No, she wouldn't let on. I didn't want to make a lot of trouble, so I didn't say anything. I mean, if you're frightened of someone, it doesn't mean they're going to kill you. But this afternoon, not long ago, Adrian Mallaby came and sat down by me, and talked to me in a friendly sort of way. He wanted to know a bit about Diana, and what I'd thought and seen when I found her. Then he asked me if I was going to the dance tonight, and he said he'd like to escort me. He was very nice, but I got scared and went and told Professor Ludlow——"

"They're not going to have another of those alarming dances?" Ludlow interrupted with a look of horror.

"I'm afraid they are," Montero said. The Captain asked me whether it was advisable in the circumstances. I told him that the most useful thing from the point of view of our investigations would be for the life of the ship to carry on as normally as possible."

"I shan't go," Julie said. "It wouldn't seem right, after Diana dying in that awful way. And I don't want to be with Adrian Mallaby. If someone else would escort me, it might be different."

She looked hard at Ludlow, who shrank but was saved in time.

"I understand how you feel, Miss West," Montero said gently, "and it does you credit. But it would be a great favour to me, and perhaps to your friend's memory, if you would go to the dance, and let Adrian Mallaby accompany you if he wants to. Don't go out on deck with him. He can't hurt you in the saloon, and we shall sit where we can watch him all the time."

"Well—if you say so, Inspector. But I don't understand."

"Nor do I yet. But we may learn something. Meanwhile, we will make sure that you are safe. And I'm sure Professor Ludlow will help us," he added slyly.

"I promise nothing, not even for the false flattery of a titular promotion," Ludlow said.

"Well, you'd better look after Miss West now, because we've got an appointment to see the Captain."

Although the Captain immediately invited them to come in when Montero knocked, he was in fact far from ready to see them. They stood self-effacingly inside the door and took in everything with the skill of long detective practice. The Captain's day-cabin looked more like an executive office than part of a ship, being furnished with some functional steel chairs, a filing cabinet and a large desk behind which the Captain himself was sitting. Those of his profession seem to lose all differences of race and origin by the time they reach high command and to take on an image of being shortish, solidly built, red-faced and inclining to loss of hair. These features, with the usual brisk but considered efficiency, were manifested in the Captain of the *Inquirer*, even though he was now occupied with one of the two telephones on his desk. Burrows was sitting near him, holding a sheaf of papers and looking apprehensively at Montero and Springer.

"What did you say her name was?" the Captain demanded of the telephone. "Mrs. Lawrence? Wait a minute." He studied a list in front of him. "Oh, yes, I've got her—Promenade Deck. Where did she lose it?—Well, if she doesn't know, how are we expected to look for it?—Yes, I know—All right, Purser, I'll do something."

He dropped the telephone on its rest.

"A Mrs. Lawrence has lost a diamond brooch, but she doesn't know where," he said to Burrows. "Why the hell do these women bring expensive jewellery to sea with them? See if any of the stewards can give you a line on it. I shan't keep you a moment," he added to the pair at the door. "Do sit down. I've just got to fix up my table for dinner tomorrow."

Burrows bristled importantly with his papers.

"Now, who have we got so far?" the Captain went on.

"Mr. and Mrs. Burmeister, sir."

"Who are they?"

"He's part of Burmeister and Spendlow, International Deodorant Enterprises."

"Good God! All right. Who else?"

"Miss Heaton, who's the niece of a former Cabinet Minister."

"So we want one more man. Any suggestions, Burrows?"

"I thought perhaps Mr. Ludlow, sir."

"Ludlow, who's he?" The Captain searched through his list. "Yes, here he is. Adam Ludlow, University Lecturer. Why him?"

"He seems a very nice gentleman, sir."

"In that case he's not likely to write to the company and complain that he was never invited to sit at my table. What University is he at?"

"London, I think."

"Uh. No, I don't think so. Let's find somebody else. Who's the Reverend Mr. Starkey?"

"I believe he's just an ordinary clergyman."

"Pity. What about—er—Dr. Willis?"

"Oh yes, a very good idea. He is in fact a hospital consultant. I'll send him your invitation, sir. That is, unless you wouldn't really like to meet Mr. Ludlow."

"Who I'd like to meet doesn't get much influence, Burrows. I've been reminded too often of what profit the company makes from the best cabins. Right, that's all for now. Thanks."

Burrows went out reluctantly, while the Captain rose and greeted his new visitors.

"Sorry to keep you waiting, gentlemen," he said. "I hate all this protocol nonsense, but it goes with the job. Now, have you had all the help you need? I gave orders that you were to be given every possible facility. By the way, which of you is which?"

"I'm Inspector Montero, sir, and this is Sergeant Springer. Yes, thank you, we've been——"

"Montero, now there's an unexpected name in the British police. Where did you get it?"

"There was a Spanish ancestor, many generations back, and the name's run on. We're a Devon family."

"Devon—a bit of the Spanish Armada, eh?"

"Actually, I think he was a pedlar, sir, who settled down and started a business in Plymouth."

"Pity. Well, I mustn't take up your time. Names are

interesting things, though. I knew a chap once whose name was Benedict Fortescue, and he was as black as your hat. He used to keep a bar in Trinidad."

"Well, if we might ask you one or two questions, sir, just briefly."

"Yes, of course. Fire away."

"Did you ever meet Miss Diana Acton, during the earlier part of the cruise?"

"Not quite. Only missed her by an hour or so, though. She had an appointment to see me on the evening she was killed. She was supposed to come at nine-thirty. Naturally, she didn't."

Springer almost bounced on his hard chair.

"Do you know why she wanted to see you, sir?" Montero asked.

"No idea. She left word that it was urgent and could be told to nobody else. They're always wanting something—losing things, wrong cabins, bad stewards—usually I push them off on Burrows or the Purser, but she was particularly keen to see me. Sometimes I wish I was back on watch-keeping. It's a damned lonely life."

"I'm sure it is, sir."

"Who killed her?" The question was abrupt, demanding an answer.

"We don't know yet, but we intend to find out. Can you give us any suggestions at all, sir?"

"Not me. I've never known such a thing happen before. Except when a Lascar fireman knifed Ma Keng two days out of Shanghai. He was the best steward I ever had. It's really upset them back in the company's office."

"We shall try to add as little as possible to the trouble. Of course, it is necessary to question the passengers——"

"All of them?"

"Only a few, I hope."

"Well, let's hope you succeed before we get to Genoa. You've got a list?"

"Yes, Mr. Burrows gave us one. Thank you, sir, we won't

disturb you any more at present."

Outside on the deck they looked at each other meaningly.

"You may be right about blackmail, Jack," Montero said, "though I still don't see why that should make *her* be killed."

A woman with orange hair accosted them as they made their way back to their own cabin and asked them whether everything was safe. They assured her that it was, with more show of confidence than either of them felt.

There are few sights more depressing than a room decorated for no reason except that somebody has decided to have some organized fun. The lights in the main saloon had not yet been lowered for the greater intimacy of dancing, and the glare was bright on festoons of coloured paper. Burrows, just visible in a small room behind the bar, was sorting out an awesome collection of small cardboard hats and large cardboard noses. The band was making experimental noises on its dais, while a few early arrivals sat self-consciously at tables and tried to look amused.

Although Ludlow was himself fairly early, he made straight for the bar and leaned his bony elbows on it with his back to the room. He may have been prompted by the need for immediate whisky without the delay of a waiter, or he may perhaps have noticed that the far corner of the bar was already occupied by David Acton. Ludlow said nothing, though Acton continued to cast glances at him at increasingly frequent intervals.

"Lot of damned nonsense," Acton suddenly said to nobody in particular.

"A great deal of our social life is," Ludlow agreed. "At this very moment, scenes of compulsory jollification similar to this are being repeated all over the world. Our increasing leisure has led us to abandon the traditional seasons of the year when rejoicing was a natural conclusion——"

"I'm talking about your detective friends." Acton interrupted him sharply and in a voice that was not quite clear. It seemed to Ludlow that he was acting like a man who wants to appear more drunk than he really is.

"What has Inspector Montero been doing to upset you?"

"I didn't say anything about upsetting me. Nothing upsets me. I'm a man who doesn't mind accepting responsibility and taking decisions. I run my own business and make a success of it. I'm not short of money—never mind what my wife told you. Have another drink."

Acton swayed slightly but recovered himself with what appeared to be very good control. Ludlow continued to watch him but said nothing.

"It's all nonsense," Acton went on after filling his own glass without again pressing his offer on Ludlow. "Diana killed herself. That's her business. Why do these flat-footed snoopers have to come round asking questions? She killed herself, and that ought to be the end of it. Can't help her now."

"Why should your sister kill herself?" Ludlow asked.

"I don't know. She never told me anything. Maybe some man she was keen on. She was always a funny girl. I wish they'd leave my wife and daughter alone. What do they know about it?"

"People sometimes know more than they themselves realize."

"That's true. God, yes, that's true. But not Theresa—she doesn't know anything. I'm afraid of what it'll do to her. I mean, she's not unbalanced or anything like that, but she's full of queer ideas. She's very like Diana in some ways. Why, she's even beginning to look like her. Haven't you noticed it?"

"I don't think I have. I'm sure you needn't worry about her, since she's basically a sensible enough girl."

"I'm glad to hear you say that. She is sensible all right. So was Diana, for things that concerned her interests. She could look after herself."

"Do you think your sister could have committed suicide because of some financial trouble—perhaps some investment that went wrong?" Ludlow said.

"Not Diana. She was as shrewd as a monkey. She never went into anything with her eyes shut. No, the money's all right. I've done a bit of checking up by phone with the solicitor—oh, there's the family. Excuse me, old man."

Looking as if he had said too much, and walking quite steadily, Acton went to join Elizabeth and Theresa who had just sat at a table near the band. Looking after him, Ludlow saw that Montero and Springer were now sitting near the door which led to the deck, in a position where they could survey the whole room. He took his drink and went over to join them. They were drinking beer, which Springer was swallowing with undisguised contempt.

"This bottled stuff isn't much good," he said accusingly as though Ludlow were somehow responsible. "The food on this boat's smashing, but they can't make a decent cup of tea and they haven't got any draught beer. I wouldn't pay to come on a holiday like this."

"Let's remember that the taxpayer is paying for both of us, so you can save your pennies and your grumbles for the sturdy Saxon pleasures of Southend. Let's see what Mr. Ludlow has to tell us," Montero said.

Ludlow told him of his short conversation with David Acton.

"He's too keen to push the suicide angle," Springer said when Ludlow had finished. "I don't trust that one, not an inch."

"Nor do I," Montero agreed. "And he admits to have been suspiciously quick on finding out about the money that might be coming to him. One thing accords with what we've learned though—that Diana Acton was a shrewd and acquisitive business-woman."

"What's that?" Ludlow asked, not wanting to miss anything.

"I'll tell you, but keep it to yourself because it's privileged communication and all that kind of thing. David Acton isn't the only one who's been ringing up the family solicitors from mid-ocean. We've been through to the number that Diana called in London—it was her solicitors, who apparently handle a good deal of her investments. She asked them to find out about the real estate company in which Julie West has so much financial interest."

"Yes, Miss West said that there was talk of it," Ludlow said. "Obviously no time was being wasted. But what was the result of her question?"

"Well, apparently they checked on this company through some contact in America. It's genuine, financially sound and likely to prosper. They recommended a fairly substantial investment, and Diana Acton promised to call back and give them definite instructions in a day or two. Of course she never did, because she was dead."

"I see." Ludlow drained his glass and looked at the bottom of it as if truth lay there. "What do you make of all that?"

"I'm beginning to wonder if there was someone who didn't want that deal to go through," Montero said.

"Like her brother for instance," said Springer, looking like a terrier who has had one bite at a rat and isn't going to miss the next chance.

"Perhaps, though it wouldn't put the money any farther away from him really. It might be somebody who didn't want fresh money to go into the company—some American rival interest perhaps. I just don't know."

"We still haven't found out what that fellow Mallaby was putting the wind up Diana about," Springer reminded him.

"Nor we have, but I hope we shall before long. He clearly had some kind of hold over her, and it might be connected with this proposed deal. Again, it might not. Hullo, here he is."

Adrian Mallaby came in, guiding Julie West by the elbow in a manner that could have been threatening rather than protective, were it not that his red face had an even broader grin than usual. Julie looked frightened, but smiled faintly when she saw the table where Ludlow and the two detectives were sitting together. Adrian took her to the far end of the saloon, to a small corner table next to one occupied by Joseph and Cornelia Grossheim. Rupert Penge had joined the Actons at their table, and seemed to be the only one showing any interest in life. David was leaning forward on the table as if half asleep, Elizabeth was pale and anxiously silent, and Theresa seemed to be indulging in one of her sullen moods. It was left to Rupert to keep up a flow of talk, which he interrupted only to give a venomous look at Adrian as he went past. The room was nearly full now, and a roll on the drum was the signal for semi-darkness, polite clapping and the first shower of paper streamers.

Burrows, smiling broadly but with an uneasy look in his eyes, announced the first dance. Montero looked relaxed, a passenger quietly enjoying the evening, but his calmness was that of a panther waiting for the chance to spring. The normal bar service was being supplemented by Harmer, who carried drinks to the tables with his usual sullen acceptance of an unjust lot. The saloon grew warm, in spite of the open windows, as the dancing became more frenetic. Ludlow extracted a fragment of paper streamer from his drink, and felt a desire for cool breezes.

"The next dance will be a snowball dance," Burrows announced loudly.

"I could do with one of them," Springer said, wiping his forehead with a large handkerchief.

"What on earth's that?" Montero whispered.

"One couple starts, then they break up and each picks a new partner, and so on; it's all very dismal," Ludlow explained.

"I congratulate you on your knowledge of modern dancing."

"One picks it up from students—a sort of process of osmosis which develops even though the will resists. I hope nobody bothers me."

Ludlow had no need to worry, for his association with the other two was enough protection against being drawn into the dance. Burrows took the floor with a perspiring woman of doubtful age but undoubted ranking in the passenger-list. Montero kept his eyes on Julie and Adrian, and the tables around them. As the number of dancing couples, increased, it became harder to see what was going on. The Grossheims were both claimed after a time. Theresa was soon taken out, until the next break when she returned and chose Rupert. During one of the breaks, when everyone on the floor was scrambling madly to find a new partner from those still sitting, Harmer took a tray to Adrian's table. Not knowing that three pairs of eyes watched every movement, he put drinks on the table and gave Adrian a pad to sign. A moment later, Elizabeth appeared, took Adrian's arm and led him off. Julie sat alone, while Montero seemed to breathe more easily.

The floor was now almost full, with only a few neglected ones still at the tables and trying to look as if they did not mind. Julie forlornly powdered her nose which, it must be admitted, was by now distinctly shiny.

"Go and ask her to dance," Montero said.

"You ask her," Ludlow replied sullenly.

They realized that they sounded like a couple of youths at a dance-hall, and both laughed. The next and final break in the dance soon came, and this time David Acton went and rescued Julie from her loneliness. The last phase was short but hectic. When the band at last stopped, in spite of the claps of those who seemed ready for even more, David returned Julie to her table and stood talking with her for a few moments. Then Adrian returned, redder and hotter than ever, and David went to rejoin his family. The Grossheims stopped for a word with Julie as they passed.

The floor cleared, and Ludlow and his companions had a perfect view of what happened. Adrian picked up a glass and swallowed its contents at a gulp. Julie's voice could be clearly heard in the comparative quietness now that the band had stopped.

"Oh, Adrian, you are an idiot—you've taken my drink," she said.

Adrian did not reply except with the beginning of a cry that was choked into a fight for breath. His eyes bulged and all the colour went from his face as if wiped away. He made a half turn and fell to the floor.

— 12 —

For the next few minutes everything seemed to happen at once. It was only later that the pattern began to emerge and the solution to appear. At a word from Montero, Springer ran to the door of the saloon and stood with his back to it. Montero pushed aside those who were already crowding round Adrian's body.

"Get the doctor," he said to Harmer, who seemed untroubled and unsurprised by events.

The doctor was already making a somewhat unsteady progress across the floor, leaving behind a faded blonde in a silver dress. Julie was screaming, not loudly but in soft, sobbing bursts, as he came and knelt heavily by the table.

"He's dead," he said, looking up at Montero. "Looks like cyanide again. I've never known two cases so close together."

Nobody felt inclined to comment on this naïve piece of experience. Burrows came and started tugging at Montero's sleeve like a child wanting attention. Julie attached herself damply to Ludlow, clinging to his lapels and reiterating, "It was meant for me. Somebody wanted to kill me."

"Can the passengers go to their cabins?" Burrows asked. "Your man won't let anybody leave."

"Yes, they can go. All right, Jack, come and give a hand over here."

There was a rush for the door when Springer left it. He came, looking inquiringly at his chief.

"Oh, let them go," Montero said. "They can't get away, except into the sea. Anyway, what's the use of interrogating anyone? We saw everything that happened. He got away with it right under our eyes."

He sounded wearier and more dispirited than Ludlow had ever heard him. Meanwhile the doctor had recovered himself sufficiently to give Julie something that had calmed her. Harmer, with a cloth and a tray, was going about his business and collecting glasses as if nothing had happened.

"Leave them glasses alone," Springer snapped as he reached for the glass from which Adrian had drunk.

"Have him moved to your surgery and do an autopsy—though there's little doubt what you'll find."

The doctor, who had not done so much work for years, looked dispirited but nodded. Montero's manner was brusque, lacking his usual disarming and sometimes misleading courtesy. He managed to speak more gently, however, when he turned to Julie.

"Miss West, I'll quite understand if you don't feel like talking tonight, but I should be very grateful if you could answer a few questions."

"Yeah, sure. I'm sorry I went off like that. But I guess it was an awful fright to realize what was in my glass," she said.

"I'm very sorry this should have happened. I feel guilty about exposing you to it, and I shan't take any more risks with your safety. But anything you can tell me now may help us to catch the person who killed Diana Acton—and tried to kill you."

Julie gulped and nodded.

"We saw most of what happened at your table all the evening," Montero said. "Will you please tell me your own impression of everything, from the time Mallaby ordered the drinks."

"Well, we'd been sitting there quite a while. He asked me what I'd have to drink. He'd been quite nice really all evening, and I wasn't feeling so scared of him as I did at the beginning. Anyway, I said I'd have a gin and lime. So he called the waiter, and he ordered one for me, and a gin and French for himself."

"Was it Harmer that took the order?" Montero asked.

"Yes, the man from the dining-room. It was during the snowball dance, and there was quite a crowd on the floor already. He brought the drinks, and Adrian signed for them, and just then Elizabeth Acton came up and took him out to dance—Adrian I mean, not Harmer. So I sat there and I didn't take a drink until he came back, but David asked me to dance in the next break. At the end of the dance he brought me to the table, and we talked for a little until Adrian came."

"All this time the drinks were on the table, untouched?" Montero asked.

"Yes. So Adrian picked up a glass and swallowed what was in it. So I reached for my drink, and then I saw it was the wrong colour. So I looked harder and realized that Adrian had taken mine instead of his own. I called out to him, but it was too late."

"How do you think he made the mistake?"

"Well, the two glasses didn't look too different, and the light wasn't very good. But I can't really see why."

"Did he come back to the table from the same side as he left?"

"Let me see—no—why, no, he didn't. He was on my right and the two glasses were put down in front of us in the way we wanted them. But then he came back from dancing on the other side, so that he was on my left. I guess he must just have picked up the glass that was nearest to him."

"So he got the gin and lime, which was poisoned. All right, Miss West. You've had a lucky escape, but it's obvious that someone is out to kill you. Why, we don't know. But perhaps you could try to think what you could possibly know about the murder of Miss Acton that somebody doesn't want repeated."

"I don't have any ideas, Inspector."

"Go to your cabin now. Have a rest, but please think hard as well. You may not realize it, but there's obviously something that makes you dangerous. Lock your cabin, and don't let anybody in except one of us. Call me on the telephone at once if you have any trouble—or any ideas."

Julie went away, and Montero looked, tight-lipped, at the others.

"So there's a murderer walking about this ship, and we've just let him get away with it," he said. "We watch one man, and he gets murdered by mistake. But anyone who's so anxious to kill Julie West isn't going to delay much longer before trying again. We've got to work fast. Here, Harmer, I want to talk to you."

Harmer put down his tray and came slowly.

"Did you take an order for two drinks from Mr. Mallaby this evening?" Montero asked.

"That's right. He called me over, ordered a gin and lime and a gin and French. I got them from the bar and took them to his table. He signed for them, in the usual way. I've still got the pad here."

"What do you mean by signing in the usual way?"

"Well, sometimes passengers pay straight out for what they have, but more often they sign for it, and it all goes on the bill at the end of the cruise."

"I see. Did you put down the drinks at all between the bar and the table?"

"No, I gave the order and the barman made the drinks, then I took them straight to the table. That's all."

"That particular table was unoccupied for a time when the drinks were on it. Did you go back to it then?"

"Why should I do that?"

"Answer my question."

"No, I didn't."

"What are you doing in here, anyway? I thought you were a dining-saloon steward."

"So I am, but one of us comes to help out in here on special nights like this. It was my turn tonight, that's all."

"All right: get on with your work."

Harmer went away, muttering. Two sailors with a stretcher were removing Adrian Mallaby's body, under the doctor's direction. Montero went over to where Burrows was leaning on the bar, pale and defeated.

"What am I going to do? What on earth am I going to do?" he demanded wildly.

"Answer a few questions, if you please," Montero said.

"But Inspector, this will ruin our reputation. Two murders and still we don't know who did it."

"Then no doubt you will be anxious to help us to find out."

"Of course—but I know nothing about it. Why was Mr. Mallaby killed?"

"Because he drank from the wrong glass. The murderer was after Miss West."

"Miss West? But that's impossible. Such a charming young lady. Who could possibly want to harm her?"

"When we know that our job will be finished."

"Really, Inspector, it's too bad. One ought to feel safe with two policemen on board. I assumed that you would be able to solve the first murder—but a second one gets committed under your nose——"

Montero went red and Springer made a growling sort of noise. It was Ludlow who restored peace by asking, in a casual way,

"Did you dance throughout that peculiar snowball game?"

"Yes," Burrows said, "I took a new partner every time. That's the idea with that dance—gets everybody on the floor and mixes people up."

"I'm sure it does. You must have passed several times by the table where Miss West and Mallaby were sitting."

"Well—I suppose so. We all kept moving, so everybody did."

"We needn't keep you any longer, Mr. Burrows," said Montero, who had recovered his outward equanimity and was not going to let Ludlow take charge.

Burrows went away, wiping his brow, and the other

three walked out on deck. A young moon hung low over the sea, throwing a long gleam of light to cross the whiteness at the ship's bow. It was a night when even the most disillusioned souls might feel a quickening of hope. But the decks were empty. No couples leaned over the rail or had found deck-chairs in hidden corners. No men walked from bow to stern, with a proud nautical roll that affirmed a lasting rulership of the waves. Between the low moon and the sea, there was death.

They stood without speaking for several minutes, looking out across the sea to the unseen coast of Italy to the north. Ludlow found his pipe and lit it.

"Anybody could have done it," Springer said at last. "Anybody in that room could have dropped the stuff in her glass when he was dancing past the table. It needn't even be one of those we had ideas about before."

"It's got to be. There just can't be two murderers on the ship, both using cyanide. No, whoever killed Diana Acton tried to kill her cabin-companion tonight." Montero spoke quietly, looking at neither of his companions.

"It seems to me," Ludlow said, "that it would need the co-operation of two people to do it that way. I know little about the cult of dancing, but it would seem to me to be most difficult to pause and drop poison into a glass without one's partner being aware of it."

"You're probably right, though it's surprising what skill people can use when they're forced to it."

"Allowing for skill, David Acton could have done it while he was standing and talking to her after the dance," Ludlow said.

"But then this chap Mallaby was threatening her—or at least putting the wind up her—and he'd been doing the same to Miss Acton. Why shouldn't he have done it when the drinks came, under the cover of signing the pad?" Springer asked.

"And then come back and swallowed the one he'd poisoned? Don't waste time, Jack. It was an easy mistake for an unsuspecting man to make, but not a man who knew that one of them was poisoned. But we still don't know how deeply Mallaby was involved in the whole thing. We've got to find out what Julie West knows—obviously something she doesn't realize. We'll have another talk with her."

Since the death of Diana, Julie had been given a cabin on the boat-deck. The three men climbed the narrow stairway which led up to it and skirted round the lifeboats which hung as mute reminders of mortality. The window of Julie's cabin was lit up, and she opened at once when Montero knocked on her door. Her face and eyes were red, but not much more than usual. Either the doctor's remedy or her own will-power had made her calm.

"I'm very sorry to trouble you again," Montero said, "but I'd like to ask you a few more things. You don't mind if Mr. Ludlow comes in?"

"Oh *no*. Please come in, and take seats. I'm sorry I don't have anything to offer you. Poor Diana always liked to have a bottle or two handy, but I don't drink much. Maybe I could ask the steward——"

"Not on our account, I assure you. Now, I'm certain that the attempt on your life tonight is directly connected with the murder of Miss Acton. You have told us everything you can remember, but there must be something in your knowledge that makes the murderer believe that you know his identity and are liable to give him away—or her, of course. I'd be grateful if you would tell me again all that happened on that day, from the time you joined Miss Acton on the sun-deck until you found her dead in the cabin. Particularly, tell me whom you saw or spoke to."

"Well, like I said, I met up with Diana about half two. We just sat in chairs and sun-bathed, and I don't remember we spoke to anyone. I think I just said hello to Rupert Penge when he went by to get a drink for Theresa. I had one myself. But we scarcely moved for hours—it's so fine and lazy out there in the sun, you just sit. Then at last we decided we'd better go and change. I do remember now, that we passed Adrian Mallaby as we left the deck. None of us said anything—I told you, Diana was scared of him and I hardly knew him then."

"What time was this?"

"Around seven. We went to our cabin and I took a shower, then we had a glass of sherry together. I went up for dinner, about ten to eight I guess, and Diana was just going to phone for a tray. I saw Professor Ludlow on deck, and sat with him until dinner. Adrian Mallaby was there when I went in. He asked me if Diana was coming, and I said she was staying down in the cabin."

"How did he react?"

"Nothing special, that I remember. I don't think he said anything. The old couple at our table came soon after. We just talked the way people do. Adrian missed out on the dessert—said he'd had enough and was going out on deck. After dinner I went down to the cabin, and—I found Diana lying on the bed. I guess I screamed, but I'm not sure. I know I ran back up the stairs, and found Professor Ludlow, and he came back with me. That's all."

"Please think very carefully. When you went to the cabin after dinner, did you see anyone at all in the corridor outside your cabin, or coming from that direction?"

"No, I'm sure there wasn't anyone. Mr. Burrows was standing in his sort of office on the main deck."

"Now I'd like you to tell me whether anybody on board this ship had any interest at all in the property business that you've just come into."

"Why, no. I don't think I've told anyone except Diana and Professor Ludlow, because he's so kind and sympathetic, you just want to tell him everything."

"A valuable quality for our purpose," Montero said dryly, while Ludlow tried not to look embarrassed and scowled alarmingly instead.

"I did tell Cornelia Grossheim, one day while we were talking together. I was kind of surprised when Diana took so much interest in it, and wanted to invest some money. I don't know such a lot about the business myself yet, but the man who looks after everything is very good and fixes it all for me."

"Thank you, Miss West. You won't want to be troubled any more tonight. Keep your door locked. But don't fail to tell me anything you can remember about that afternoon and evening, however trivial it may seem."

"I surely will, Inspector."

They stood outside on the boat-deck and looked gloomy.

"We're not much farther on," Montero said. "Give me your notes, Jack. I'm going to talk things over with Mr. Ludlow. If we don't get this cleared up soon, we're going to be in trouble. Now you can go and fulfil one of your ambitions by asking David Acton to explain how his prints came to be on the tray and on the cabin door. Whether he's guilty or not, he must know something more than he's told us."

"Can I put the frighteners on him, sir?" Springer asked eagerly.

"You can do practically anything short of hitting him. Just remember that you're not driving a Z-car."

Torn between a sense of social hierarchy and a desire to stand well with the investigating police, Burrows had ended by giving Montero and Springer a moderately good cabin. It was here that Montero now sat looking through the notes, while Ludlow smoked his pipe and was unusually quiet.

"They've got to be connected," Montero said. "They've just got to be. And I'm sure money is at the bottom of it. Somebody didn't want Diana's money to go into this American company. Do you agree?"

"I think the two murders were done by the same person, and that money is probably the basic motive," Ludlow said. "I doubt whether we shall get very far by pursuing obvious motives, however. In my opinion, this is a case where the motive won't be proved until we have found the murderer by other means. These improbabilities often occur. When we now read of some of the concealed motives and secret relationships that are revealed in the last chapters of some Victorian novels, we are inclined to dismiss them as parts of an outworn literary convention. Yet art begins by imitating nature, and if we are prepared to grant that——"

"All right, I'm with you but we haven't time for a lecture. What did you mean by the obvious motives?"

"For instance, David Acton, who is even now being threatened by Sergeant Springer. He inherits a good deal of money. But he would be unlikely to wait until he was on a ship, in rather restricted and overlooked circumstances, before deciding to murder his sister through an unexpected opportunity. He could have arranged it more neatly at home."

"But suppose he knew that she was intending to put a large sum into this American business, and he had information that it was likely to be lost?"

"The family solicitors seemed to think it would be safe enough."

"Yes. So you think we can cut out David Acton?"

"I'm not sure yet."

"I wonder if there's something bigger in all this than we've reckoned with. There might be some international interests. I wish we knew more about this property of Julie West's."

"The silly girl doesn't seem to know much about it herself. There seems to be little risk of international complications in what is apparently known as real estate. I don't see what use unreal estate would be to anybody. However. Of course, they might have found something that even she doesn't know about. Perhaps oil."

"Or uranium. Now I wonder—no, it's too fanciful. So in fact you've no ideas?"

"I didn't say that," Ludlow said haughtily. "I was modest enough to say that I wasn't sure. But there is one very interesting factor which runs through the evidence that we have gathered so far."

"And what's that?"

"I don't think I'll commit myself just yet."

Detective-Sergeant Springer knocked on the door of the Actons' cabin with a force composed of exasperation and practice gained years ago as a uniformed constable. After some delay, David Acton opened the door and glared at him.

"What the devil do you want?"

"Can I come in and ask you a few questions?"

"No, you can't. My wife's very upset. I'm not going to have her persecuted any more."

""Then perhaps you'll step outside and talk to me here."

"I'll do nothing of the kind. I've told you all I know, and you can't connect me in any way with what happened tonight."

"I didn't say anything about tonight. The evidence which we have is concerned entirely with your sister's death. If you wish to volunteer a statement about the murder of Adrian Mallaby, perhaps I ought first to caution you that——"

"What evidence?" David asked, looking less sure of himself.

"Evidence that you handled the tray that was brought to your sister's cabin, and which you denied having seen."

David went white and came out into the corridor, shutting the door behind him.

"Are you calling me a liar?" he asked.

"Yes, Mr. Acton, I am. That is, if you persist in your story that when you went to your own cabin during dinner, there was no tray outside the other door."

"That's the truth."

"Then you interfered with it earlier, as soon as the stewardess had left it there."

"I never touched it. My wife and I went up to dinner soon after it was brought. It had been taken in when I came down during dinner."

"How can you account for the fact that your fingerprints are on the bottom of the tray?"

"That's impossible," David said faintly.

"There's no doubt about it. And your prints are also on the door of the cabin. What do you say to that?"

"I never touched the tray. I went into Diana's cabin at other times of course, so I may have left an impression on the door. Perhaps the tray was one that I'd had on deck previously—yes, that must be it. We've had drinks and things sent out to us more than once."

"Bit of a coincidence I think, Mr. Acton. And those trays get washed and polished after they've been used."

"Then you must have made a mistake."

"We don't make mistakes, Mr. Acton. And that's something which a lot of people have found out. Would you like to give any other explanation?"

"I've nothing more to say. If you can't believe that I'm innocent, try to prove that I'm not, and be damned to you."

Acton disappeared into his cabin and slammed the door. Springer went away, looking pleased with himself, and reported back to his chief.

"So he's properly rattled about something," he concluded.

"As he well might be," Montero said. "We've really got enough to charge him as it is. I'll ask the Captain to see that he's not issued with a landing-card when we dock at Naples. And it might be as well if Miss West didn't go ashore either. Whoever it was that tried to kill her tonight is likely to have another go. We can keep an eye on her better if she stays on board. You don't look very pleased about it, Mr. Ludlow. Were you looking forward to showing her the sights of Naples?"

"You policemen always impute the lowest motives to everyone," Ludlow said. "I suppose it's the result of consorting with criminals. I can't think why I ever attempt to help you. I was just thinking that we might learn something if we let her go on shore, and waited to see what happens."

"You mean use her as a sort of bait? A bit risky, though someone ought to be able to see she's safe, as long as we're prepared for trouble. Not that we made a very good job of it tonight, though. Bad luck on Mallaby, even though he does seem to have had something shady about him."

"I must go and get my sleep," said Ludlow, rising. "I'm supposed to be on holiday. All this is most upsetting and fatiguing."

"Shall we turn in, sir?" Springer asked after Ludlow had gone. "I don't reckon we can do much more tonight."

"There's one thing we've got to do—find out whether Mallaby is able to tell us more now that he's dead than he did when he was alive. At least we'll be able to get his dabs now, and maybe learn why he wasn't willing to give them. Give me the stuff and I'll go along to the doctor's place."

"I'll do it, sir," Springer said. "It'll be a nasty sort of job."

"That's why I'm going to do it myself. Get the key of his cabin from Burrows and start going over it. If young Mr. Penge is there, he'll just have to put up with it."

"I hope he is. I never cared much for them barristers. Twisty lot of blokes, if you ask me."

— 13 —

There were few people awake when the *Inquirer* passed through the Straits of Messina in the early hours of the following morning. Or it might be more accurate to say that there were few people on deck to see the dark coasts of Italy and Sicily. Some of the passengers, and one in particular, must have slept little that night. Ludlow was in the small writing-room after breakfast, resentfully writing postcards to people who had been forgotten in Greece, when Sergeant Springer tracked him down. There was an eager look on Springer's face, as if he had some very important information to give.

"Good morning, Mr. Ludlow," he said brightly.

"Morning. What's the postal district for Earls Court?"

"S.W.5. I say, I've learnt something since last night."

"Really? What is it?" Ludlow put down his pen.

"Inspector Montero snores something awful. Making the whole cabin shake, he was. What with that and the engines, I haven't had such a rotten night for years."

Further revelations were prevented by the arrival of the Inspector himself, with something more pertinent to the case.

"Well, we've found out who Adrian Mallaby really was," he announced. "We didn't even have to wait to get his prints sent back to the Yard. There were plenty of papers to tell us all we wanted—including a false passport."

"How do they get such things?" Ludlow asked. "When an honest man tries to get a passport he's treated like a criminal, but apparently some people can have as many as they want."

"It's easy enough if you have the right contacts—and the money. I suppose what we found was his real passport, and the one he presented here was the false one. Anyway, his real name was Albert Marsh and he was a pretty bad lot. He'd lived on his wits as a confidence trickster, with a bit of blackmail on the side. With the vanity of the habitual criminal, he'd obligingly kept cuttings of some of his more celebrated cases."

"I knew I'd seen him before," said Springer. "Probably it was his picture, in Records. He'd been in the nick three times. So it's no wonder he wasn't going to let us take his dabs."

Ludlow looked very thoughtful. He picked up his unfinished postcards and put them in his pocket, then settled back for a long conversation.

"It's interesting that he kept his real initials for his alias," he said.

"That's common enough. It helps to work up confidence, if you have your initials freely displayed on your luggage. A crook doesn't want to have to get a new set of luggage every time he puts on a false personality."

"Did Mallaby—or Marsh—travel a great deal?"

"His special line was ships and foreign hotels. It's a familiar business, and pays off well now that currency restrictions are almost gone. It's surprising how people who are shrewd enough at home will be taken in when they're on holiday. It may be the general feeling of relaxation and not caring, or it may be part of the easier intimacy and trust you feel with another Englishman when you're abroad. Anyway, three or four successful tricks can keep a man comfortable for the rest of the year."

"What sort of tricks do they work?"

"There's no end to the variations, but basically they play on people's wish to get something for nothing. We often say, 'You can't con an honest man.' Maybe that's why some of the smartest business-men fall for it. The victim often won't bring a charge, because he's ashamed of being taken in so easily. The main thing is to get your victim to trust you, while you work him up to expect quick profits."

"Surely it's difficult to do that with a complete stranger?"

"Not for an experienced con-man. A favourite trick is to let the mug walk around with your wallet in his pocket for a day: of course it's stuffed full of dud notes, in case he makes a break with it. Then you ask him to let you do the same with his, so that you prove good faith in each other before the big deal—then you disappear. That's pretty small-time stuff, though. People like Mallaby work on an international scale, with contacts everywhere. The whole thing makes up one of the biggest businesses in Europe—and it's not taxed."

"That's very interesting. Of course, the same kind of thing has been going on for centuries. There are some sixteenth-century pamphlets which expose very similar tricks. One of the most frequent devices for getting money——"

"But we're no nearer solving the case we're supposed to be working on," Springer said plaintively, knowing from past experience what was likely to happen when his chief started a literary discussion with Ludlow.

"Let's see what we've got," Montero said, recalled to duty. "Now we can explain why Mallaby—as we may as well call him for the time being—was so busily cultivating Miss Acton, and why she was scared of him. He was working a nice bit of blackmail, but there's no indication yet of what she had to hide."

"But that doesn't help, sir," said Springer. "I mean, a blackmailer doesn't murder his victim, it's the other way round. Unless she could possibly have had something on him and turned the tables."

"Or unless she was going to expose him. But then why was she so scared of him? And anyway, Mallaby was too smart to leave much chance of that. Besides, it's beyond reason to suppose that he was so clumsy as to poison himself instead of Miss West."

"We might have two murderers—Mallaby and somebody who tried to kill Miss West but got him instead."

"Occam's razor," Ludlow said severely, apparently to the ceiling.

"Pardon?" said Springer.

"Keep calm, Jack. Mr. Ludlow means that we oughtn't to complicate things by looking for more than one murderer, and I agree with him. We've got to find who on this ship had reasons for getting rid of those two girls. It's as simple as that, and as difficult. And we've got twenty-four hours to do it, otherwise we're going to have an awful lot of trouble."

Springer coughed, in an exploratory sort of way. It was a signal which Montero knew well.

"Is there any chance that Miss West was meant to be the first victim? I mean, suppose the murderer thought that tray was meant for her. Then he had to try again at the dance——"

"And missed again? Sorry, Jack, but I don't think much of it."

"Neither do I, sir," Springer agreed sadly.

"No, I don't think Miss West comes into the picture until after the first murder. She holds the clue to the killer, and she doesn't know it."

"There was that time she found the American fellow in the cabin, up to no good. Not much of a motive, though."

"That reminds me," Montero said to Ludlow, "we had a visit from Cornelia Grossheim this morning—long before you were up, of course. She told us that she'd seen Theresa Acton bending over the tray and examining it, while it was outside the door."

"What time?"

"She didn't know exactly, but it must have been after dinner started and the others had gone up. You remember telling us that Theresa arrived late in the dining-saloon."

"I thought Mrs. Grossheim was in a deep sleep induced by the loving power of science, which now gives us tablets to send us to sleep and other tablets to wake us up, and no doubt others to——"

"Yes, yes. Well, apparently she hadn't fully settled down, when she heard somebody moving about outside and went to investigate. I don't know why she didn't tell us before, and anyway it's a natural enough thing for a girl like Theresa to do. It's no good building much on it. So all in all, we're no further forward."

"I think we are. Did you get anything useful from David Acton last night?" Ludlow asked.

"He won't talk—yet. We're going to see him again, and we'll see him alone. He's just in the mood to make a fuss about anything, and he'd probably object to your being there."

"All right. I'll go and sit in the sun, probably for the last time this year. I've enjoyed our conversation—most interesting, really most interesting and informative."

Ludlow ambled away. Springer looked after him with apparent disappointment.

"He's not trying," he said. "He hasn't got his heart in it."

"You can't blame him, Jack. After all he is supposed to be on holiday. It's our job and we'd better get on with it. Find David Acton and bring him down to our cabin. I've got the stuff there to show him."

"Is he our man, sir?"

"He's the most likely suspect at present but I won't go farther than that."

While he waited in the cabin for Springer to return, Montero read for the twentieth time the report from the police laboratory in Valetta. He looked for a long time at one section with a puzzled frown that cleared only when David Acton was brought in. The truculence of the previous night had vanished. It was obvious that he had not slept, and that Springer's brief questioning had not been in vain. He almost lurched towards Montero and leaned forward with his hands on the table behind which the Inspector was sitting.

"I want to make a statement," he said.

"Very well, Mr. Acton. This is a voluntary statement and no record will be made of it. If, after you have told me what you want to say, it is necessary to make any charge against you, I shall caution you before allowing you to repeat or add to whatever you may have said. It's very wise of you to tell us the truth now."

"Yes, I can see that it's no good pretending that I never touched the tray. The only thing is whether you'll believe me when I tell you the truth."

Montero said nothing. David gulped, looked around as if for some last-minute refuge, then went on.

"When I left the dining-room that evening it was with the intention of seeing my sister. It seemed a good opportunity, since she was alone in her cabin and everybody else was at dinner. During the day it was almost impossible to see her by herself—she was always with that fellow Mallaby, and all the afternoon she'd been with Julie."

"What did you want to see her about?"

"I wanted money. My business needed it, desperately."

"So desperately that it couldn't wait till the end of your holiday?"

"There were—well, urgent debts. I'd been on the telephone to my manager earlier in the day. If Diana had only agreed to transfer a little money, it would have tided us over. I thought if I saw her alone, I could persuade her. You won't believe this, Inspector, I can see by your face. You can't realize that this sort of thing goes on in a family—a brother having to beg his sister for money that was his by right——" David looked as if he was breaking down.

"I can believe quite a lot that would surprise you, sir," Montero said comfortably. "Just go on with your story. Did you discuss all this with your wife and daughter?"

"Elizabeth and I talked about it at the beginning of dinner, after we'd heard that Diana wasn't coming up. I didn't say anything after Theresa came, because she isn't much help. After a time, I just said I was going down to see how Diana was, and if she wanted anything. I left the dining-room quite openly, you know."

"Yes, we know. Did you go straight to her cabin?"

"Yes, I saw that the tray was still outside the door, and I thought I'd take it in to her. I picked it up and knocked on the door."

"How did you manage all that?" Springer asked.

"What? Oh, I see. Yes, I balanced the tray on one hand, as a waiter does, and knocked. She didn't answer, so I tried the door and it was locked."

"Are you quite sure of that?" said Montero, with new interest.

"Of course. I pushed hard on the door, and called her name two or three times. But I thought she just didn't want to see me, and went away."

"Did you hear any movement inside the cabin?"

"Nothing at all."

"Not the sound of running water, perhaps?"

"No. Oh, you mean she might have been having a shower and didn't hear me? Yes, that's quite possible, though I didn't hear anything."

"Did you interfere with the tray or anything on it?"

"No, I simply picked it up and put it down. I didn't even look to see what was on it. You've got to believe me—I know how bad all this looks, but I've told you everything. I was afraid before, but now that you've found the fingerprints—you do believe me, don't you?"

"I'll ask the questions for the time being, Mr. Acton. Now perhaps you'd be kind enough to do a piece of formal identification, which is why I asked you to come."

"What—why, you—you tricked me into talking." David's face was wet and he passed his hand over it helplessly.

"Now, sir, that's a very unkind thing to say. You volunteered a statement before I was able to say anything at all, and I've had the patience to listen to it. Now I have here the box in which your sister kept her jewellery, and which she removed from the ship's safe not long before she was murdered. I'd like you to tell me if you recognize all the pieces and whether you know of any that ought to be here but are missing."

Springer produced the jewel-box. Shaking with rage, or perhaps with some other emotion, David opened it. He took out one by one the necklaces, rings and other things that it contained. Nobody spoke, while he examined each piece in turn, building up two separate piles on the table.

"These are my sister's," he said, indicating the larger pile. "I don't think there's anything missing, but I can't be sure exactly what she brought with her."

"I see. And what about these?" Montero pointed to the rest.

"I've never seen them before."

"But Miss Acton might have bought them without your knowledge?"

"She'd never have bought stuff like this. Jewellery was one of Diana's passions, and one of her greatest extravagances."

"I'm not sure that I follow you, sir."

"This stuff is worthless, Inspector. It's all paste—quite a good type of imitation, but the whole lot isn't worth more than fifty pounds."

Montero grabbed what appeared to be a diamond necklace, and looked at it for a long time through a magnifying-glass which he produced in the best Holmes manner. He sighed and looked almost sheepish.

"You're right, Mr. Acton. We ought to have spotted it ourselves—though of course we had no reason to pick out some of the stuff for a special look. I congratulate you on your skill."

David smiled without humour, and said nothing. There was a timid knock on the door, and Springer went to open it. Elizabeth Acton was outside.

"I had to come," she said. "I'm sorry, David—I promised I'd stay away, but you were so long, and I was frightened. What's happened?"

"Come in, Mrs. Acton," Montero said genially. "There's

no need to be frightened of anything."

"Have you arrested him?" Elizabeth stumbled into the cabin and dropped into a chair which Springer placed for her.

"Now really, Elizabeth——" David began.

"We haven't arrested anybody yet. But now that you're here, perhaps you wouldn't mind answering a few questions. Will you give me *your* account of why your husband left dinner on the night his sister was killed?"

David started to protest again, but thought better of it, and fell sulkily silent. Elizabeth, speaking falteringly but clearly, repeated what David had already said. Montero seemed satisfied.

"By the way, Mrs. Acton," he said when Elizabeth had finished, "do you possess much jewellery?"

"Very little. Most of it's imitation anyway—we've never been able to afford good things."

"Do you see any of your jewellery here now?"

Elizabeth looked at the table and shook her head.

"Some of that is Diana's. I've never seen the rest of it—it's certainly not mine."

"All right. I needn't keep either of you any longer at present."

After David and Elizabeth had gone, Springer looked anxiously and a little reproachfully at Montero.

"I thought you were going to tell him he couldn't go on shore this afternoon," he said.

"I've changed my mind. He can't get far if he tries to run for it, because his passport will be on the ship."

"He might have a false one, sir. We were just telling Mr. Ludlow how easy it is."

"I don't think Acton's a professional criminal, whatever he may be. In any case, he won't get away because he'll have you watching him all the time. Get the idea?"

"I'll see he doesn't give us the slip."

"Somehow I don't think he'll try. It's pretty obvious by now that the murderer is less concerned with making his escape than with silencing Julie West. She's the one who holds the answer, and she doesn't know what it is. We'll keep her on board, so there'll be no danger to her. If Acton—or anyone else for that matter—acts suspiciously, you'll be on hand to see it. But don't take any action unless you have to. I want them all back on board tonight, without any suspicions aroused. Clear?"

"Right, sir. Do you think this morning's work has given us anything new to go on, because I'm blowed if I can see it."

"Well, what have we got? Diana Acton was in possession of a good deal of fake jewellery, as well as the real and valuable stuff. She withdrew the whole lot from the ship's safe and kept it in her cabin. At the same time she was associating with a man who's turned out to be a professional swindler and blackmailer. What does it look like to you?"

"I don't know, but it does look like more than somebody getting jealous of a bit of lovemaking. Do you think we're on to something big, sir?"

"We may be at that. The whole Acton family might repay a bit of careful checking up. We shan't be able to do that properly till we're back at the Yard—but I'm going to do some telephoning from Naples this afternoon. If there was anything to show a previous association between her and Mallaby, or Marsh, or whatever his real name was—but that wouldn't help much, because he's dead. Come on, let's go and clear our heads on deck."

"That's most interesting," Ludlow said, when they had found him in the bar and given him the latest news.

"Does it make any sense to you?"

"Oh, yes. Everything points to the same conclusion. There's only one possible answer."

"Well, would you mind telling me what you think it is, or is that asking too much from a distinguished academic?" Montero asked.

"Sarcasm doesn't suit you. I'd like a little more proof before I say anything. In fact, you've got all the facts in front of you. Admittedly, I know one thing which you may not, though you've had every chance of finding it for yourself. But even without that——"

"All right, all right. Are you going ashore this afternoon?"

"I think I will. Naples is to my mind one of the less attractive Mediterranean towns, though no doubt opinions differ. The best thing about it is the appproach by sea. Still, this visit may turn out to be instructive, if you'd relent and let Julie West come too."

"I suppose she'll be all right if she keeps with the others." Montero looked hard at him.

"I just want to see what happens. Quite possibly, nothing will. But if your sergeant is there, she'll be all right."

"Thanks very much, but I've got to watch that bloke Acton," Springer said.

"I'm sure you can manage both. I'll keep close to her all the time."

"That will please her a lot," Montero said. "All right, but bring her back safely."

— 14 —

Whether Ludlow was right or wrong in his general opinion of Naples, he was certainly right about the beauty of its bay. The rails of the *Inquirer* were lined with passengers, as the blue haze of the coastline gradually took shape and revealed the town that rose shiningly out of the sea. Fortified by yet another good lunch, Ludlow leaned and smoked his pipe and pretended to be unaware that Rupert Penge was standing next to him. Theresa was nowhere in sight, which was unusual in itself; and Penge seemed nervously unsure, which was even more unusual.

"Only one more day to go," came a rather cracked voice at last.

"Eh? Oh, Penge, I didn't notice you. Yes, we'll be sailing into Genoa this time tomorrow. The Gulf of Spezia, where Shelley was drowned. What a tragic crowd they were, the young Romantics. Yet perhaps the most tragic of them all came from the first generation. You will recall Browning's poem about Wordsworth, where he sees the old man who outlived all his first ideals——"

"I want to talk to you," Rupert said desperately.

"Go ahead, my dear fellow. I'd be most interested to hear your evaluation of Wordsworth, since the modern fashion of criticism——"

"This is something rather more serious," Rupert said.

Ludlow looked disapprovingly at the suggestion that there was anything more serious than poetry, but then contrived to smile encouragingly. Feeling for words, anxious for advice, Rupert looked a much younger and more appealing creature than he had during the past week.

"You'll keep this to yourself?" he asked.

"I can't promise that until I know what it is. If it doesn't help towards solving the things that have been happening on this ship, I'll most certainly respect your confidence. If it does, then the sooner it is said, the better for everyone. Yes, for everyone."

Rupert said nothing for a time, but gazed across the narrowing stretch of water between the ship and the shore, almost as if he expected to see some refuge on the other side. When he spoke again, he did not look at Ludlow.

"It's about the poison," he said.

"Yes?" Ludlow's tone was interested but not excited.

"The stuff that Theresa had. It was only for a joke. She likes to do crazy things, but she's a fine girl really. She wouldn't show it, but she's very upset that it should have been used like this."

"It seems unlikely that it should have been used at all." Ludlow continued to look out across the bay.

"What do you mean? It was cyanide, wasn't it, that killed Diana? And cyanide that was used to try and poison Julie West?"

"Undoubtedly. But I understand that the particular batch of cyanide which you're concerned about was discreetly thrown overboard before either of the murders was committed."

"That's just it. She didn't throw it away—she lost it."

At last Ludlow turned away from the sea. He leaned back on the rail, his hands gripping it with an intensity that showed the excitement rising in him. His expression was still urbane.

"You'd better tell me," he said.

"Yes." Rupert nodded. "I've been worrying about it for days. Theresa told her mother that she'd got rid of the stuff, just after we left Athens. In fact she didn't do anything about it then. It was on the afternoon of the day when Diana was killed that I persuaded her that she ought not to leave it there any longer."

"Just a minute. Leave it where?"

"In the cabin—the first one, that she'd shared with Diana. When she moved out after the first night, everything was in a bit of a flap, and she just left it behind. She's rather scatter-brained, I'm afraid."

"Where exactly was it?"

"In the bathroom cabinet. Well, that afternoon I asked her if she'd really got rid of it, and she admitted that she'd never gone back for it. I told her that she must do something about it. I managed to convince her—I find that she's quite easy to handle if you go about it the right way."

Rupert smirked and looked unpleasantly like himself. The shore was quite near now; the white houses had grown windows and balconies, and trees sprouted along the promenade.

"What happened?" Ludlow demanded abruptly.

"Well, she agreed to go and try to get it, and throw it away. We could see that Diana and Julie were together on the sun-deck, so it was just a question of whether the cabin would be unlocked. It was, but she couldn't find the tin of poison. It wasn't where she had left it, and there was no sign of it. Then, a few hours later—you know what happened."

"Yes. I want you to tell the Inspector all this. You should have gone to him before."

"It will look bad for Theresa though, won't it?"

"Not as bad as it will look if the poison still turns up—as it may well do when the ship is being prepared for the next voyage—and nothing has been said. Go and find him now, before we dock."

When Ludlow takes this tone, young men usually obey him. Rupert went off obediently to tell his story. By the time he reappeared, the *Inquirer* was safely berthed and the tourists were beginning to pour down the gangway. Ludlow waved his landing-card at the Italian policeman on duty and hastened with long strides across the quay, through the customs sheds and out into the blinding sunlight of the square beyond. Sweeping aside the assembly of touts for hotels, taxis and brothels, he arrived panting at a sleek blue motor-coach and climbed in. Julie West was pleasantly surprised when he sat down heavily next to her and draped his long legs into position as well as he could.

"These Italian coaches appear to be built for dwarfs," he announced.

"I'll try to make more room," Julie said, squeezing herself nearer the window.

"Not at all, it was just a general observation."

"Have you been here before, Professor Ludlow?"

"Yes, years ago."

"Oh, good, you'll be able to tell me all about it."

Ludlow never minds telling anyone all about it, and he was also anxious to keep Julie under observation the whole time. He was deep in medieval history by the time a dark Neapolitan guide mounted the coach and blew into a hand-microphone. In the back seat, Springer breathed down David Acton's neck and looked with Anglo-Saxon disapproval at the whole situation.

They drove along the white promenade by the edge of the sea, gazing at the twin cones of Vesuvius through a shining haze of sunlight. The shrill cries of the modern city drowned the ghostly voices of Pompeii and challenged the shadow of more recent deaths that hung over some of the passengers in the coach. Then through narrow streets, past stalls of fruit and fish displayed unhealthily but excitingly in the sun, they mounted to the heights above the city. Obedient as sheep, they decanted themselves from the coach and followed the guide.

"Here behold the panoramic vista of Napoli," the guide said in a bored sort of way.

They stood and beheld, but two of them at least had only one eye for the beauty that stretched on all sides. Ludlow hovered by Julie West, with a fervour which was no doubt arousing all kinds of unintended reactions in her. Springer, more experienced in this sort of thing, contrived to look casual but never let David out of his sight.

In and out of the crowd there darted little men anxious to sell watches, postcards, fountain pens and necklaces.

"See, gold," said a flash of white teeth at Ludlow's elbow.

"I have a perfectly good watch, thank you," Ludlow said politely.

"Gold. Ten thousand lire. Very cheap."

"It can't possibly be gold at that price, and I don't want it anyway."

"See, good pen. Gold. Five thousand lire."

"I don't want a gold pen; I'm not an American film producer."

"Lady, see, very pretty. Gold. You try."

This particular little man was later to disappear, and it was never established whether he was a deliberate accomplice or was merely pursuing his normal trade. He is probably pursuing it still. What happened next was sudden and was made easier by the fact that the crowd was now fairly large. The coach-loads from the *Inquirer* had been joined by another group. Julie was bending her head to look at the brooch which was about to be pinned on her dress, and Ludlow was trying to shoo away the hawker. One moment there seemed to be nobody near them, then a man darted out of the crowd, grabbed Julie's bag and gave her a push which landed her neatly in Ludlow's arms.

The thief ran across the open space behind them and seemed to vanish into the ground. In fact he had darted into a very narrow passage between two of the shops which were competing energetically for business with the street vendors. Springer followed him, with a speed which spoke highly for the general fitness of the Metropolitan C.I.D. In spite of his London clothes and heavy shoes, he was out of sight through the narrow entrance only a few seconds after his quarry. Disengaging himself from the wailing Julie, Ludlow followed much more slowly, but with a speed which surprised himself.

The passage ran between blank walls for about thirty

yards. A moment later, and the thief could have disappeared into any one of a network of doorways, cellar openings and side alleys. But Springer, with his coat flying behind him, performed a quick sliding tackle and then started to let off some of the frustration which had been mounting in him since he left his beloved London. Ludlow stood and looked pensively at the two of them, and made a few encouraging and congratulatory noises. Rupert Penge appeared slowly at the entrance to the passage, assessed the situation, and ran forward with a great show of rolling up his sleeves and rubbing his fist.

Springer and his captive came back into the sunlight, to be surrounded by a crowd of voluble Neapolitans. The tourists stood at a distance and added the spectacle to their store of holiday experiences.

"Move along there, please," said Springer, breathing heavily. "No loitering, please. Fetch one of the local coppers, somebody. Here, get a policeman will you—you know, gendarme—toot sweet. Blimey, anybody speaka da English?"

One of the guides appeared, offered help and was sent to telephone for a police car. The thief, having soon discovered that there was no hope of slipping away from Springer's expert grip, began to protest his innocence in loud and operatic tones. It was fortunate that Springer was not able to understand what exactly was being said about him, his personal tastes and habits, and the elaborate details of his ancestry. Meanwhile Ludlow returned Julie's bag and assured himself that she was all right.

"Is anything missing?" he asked.

"I don't think so." Julie fished inside. "I don't have much here, although it's quite a big purse to carry. I thought maybe I'd buy some souvenirs in the town. No, I guess he didn't have time to take anything."

"Is there anything there that could be specially wanted—I mean anything apart from money?"

"Why no. Oh, do you think he was after me, not just taking a chance like an ordinary thief?"

"It looks like it. Otherwise, why should he have come through to you, when he could have snatched something on the edge of the crowd? Still, there's no harm done and perhaps he'll be able to tell the police something useful."

"Oh, I don't want the poor man to get into trouble. As you say, there's no harm done. And there's such awful poverty here—maybe he was just trying to get money for his family. Can't they let him go and forget about it?"

Ludlow looked round and saw that there was nobody near. Nevertheless, he drew Julie a little farther apart before speaking.

"I don't want to alarm you," he said, "but I'm afraid there's no doubt that you were singled out for attack, and that it's connected with all that's been happening on the ship. When the local police have found out who was employing this man, I think we shall be near a solution. I don't think you are going to be in any more danger, but keep close to me until we are back on board."

A black police car screeched into the space in front of the shops, scattering tourists and residents with a fine impartiality. There was an impassioned conversation, interpreted by the guide. It appeared that the thief was well known, and that there would be no difficulty in persuading him to talk. None of the ladies and gentlemen need inconvenience themselves further. Springer gave and received a few necessary particulars, and the car drove away with renewed recklessness.

The rest of the afternoon's tour seemed an anticlimax. Those who profited most from the incident were the postcard-sellers, since accounts had to be penned and posted at once. Those at home had to be prepared for the coming recital of what had happened in Naples: the encounter with a desperate gang of criminals, the thrilling chase, the hero from Scotland Yard who had upheld the best British traditions.

Springer himself looked like a rather lean cat which had found a window open in a dairy. On the way back, he confided to Ludlow that it was the best arrest he had made for a long time "and without the bother of taking a statement afterwards." Julie was pale but cheerful and now seemed inclined to take the whole thing in the true tourist spirit.

"But what the devil did he want her bag for?" Montero said two hours later as the *Inquirer* sailed out of the Bay of Naples and headed north towards Genoa. "I've been through its contents with her, and there's nothing that can possibly have any bearing on either of the murders."

"I don't agree." Ludlow was complacent as he drank his Campari and soda. "There are no gaps left to fill in now, though the Naples police may be able to give some confirmation."

Montero nodded, more in scepticism than agreement.

"They know the fellow all right," he said. "He's got a record as long as your arm for snatching bags and picking pockets. But he doesn't generally take such a risk as he did today. If he was working for somebody, then we might get farther forward. Anyway, if they find out anything, the wires will be humming between Naples and Genoa; we'll make contact with the police there when we land tomorrow. I only hope we'll have some results too."

"Oh, we shall. Let's start at the end and work backwards," Ludlow said.

"Do you mean that the murder of Mallaby is the real crime, and the other was more or less accidental? We've been assuming that it was the other way round."

"Not exactly. But it's the second murder which opens the first crack, so to speak. I'll enlighten you after dinner. Before we dine, is there anything more that you've learnt today, by way of hors-d'œuvres?"

"Yes, there is. Just before you went on shore, Rupert Penge came to see me."

"And I know what he told you. It was on my advice," Ludlow said complacently.

"Well, what do you think of it?"

"Only that a lot of people could have got access to the

poison. Since the poison was undoubtedly used, and was a type not difficult to obtain, I don't think we gain a great deal. Is that the sum of your day's work? It seems to me that you've just been lazing about, while I have been climbing the hot and odorous streets of Naples, fighting with Italian gangsters——"

"Blimey, you never got near him," Springer said indignantly.

"Quiet, both of you. Yes, between naps I did do quite a lot of work. For one thing, I went through the pathologist's report again. His estimate of the amount of time the orange juice had been in the stomach would put death long before it is known to have happened. I mean, we've overwhelming evidence that Diana Acton was alive until about ten minutes before dinner, and that she was dead by the end of it. How could she have swallowed the stuff an hour earlier and then walked off to her cabin in sight of everyone, and had sherry?"

"Quite easily," Ludlow allowed himself a slight chuckle then looked severely as if someone were trying to catch him out.

"Was there some kind of substitution? But who——?"

"I'll tell you after dinner. Is there anything else?"

"Yes, you infuriating old don. I had another word with Elizabeth Acton, when she came back on board after the trip. She was, you remember, with Adrian Mallaby, alias Marsh, during part of that snowball dance. She's positive that he couldn't have dropped anything into the glass when they passed the table. I had wondered whether he'd done it, and hit his own glass by mistake, though it seemed incredible that a man should take such a risk in the semi-dark. I also asked her to think of what he had said during that dance. One thing was interesting.

"What was it?"

"She asked him how he was enjoying the cruise. He said that he thought it was going to be a profitable one for him. Now, that fits in very well with what we now know about his activities, but does it get us any further?"

"It makes the whole thing neater. Yes, very good."

"I also asked her why Diana could possibly have arranged to see the Captain on the night she was killed. But there was no clue to that. So there we are. Have you got any ideas, Jack? You're very quiet over that beer—though I must say that you've done a good enough job today to deserve a rest."

Springer looked up, with a thoughtful expression on his long, melancholy face.

"There is one thing, sir," he said. "I've been thinking about who could have got to the poison most easily. Now that American chap, Grossheim—he was in the cabin with Diana on the very evening that Theresa moved out and Julie West moved in. In fact, she caught them snogging. He could have got hold of the stuff then, and had a motive for getting rid of both the girls. Oh, I know it's nothing much as it appears, but suppose he had some interest in this bit of property company in America. Suppose he and Mallaby were doing some kind of deal to get control of it. Well, just suppose."

"Suppose we go and have dinner," Montero said, "and then go to Mr. Ludlow's seminar on criminal detection."

— 15 —

On the last day of a cruise, the ship seems to have sailed into a different world. The passengers who have been lying about for days in the briefest of sportswear now emerge well groomed and heavily dressed for the end of their journeys. It is difficult to recognize those who, first glimpsed uncomprehendingly in the customs-house, have since been transformed into airy creatures of light and water. Now the circle is completed, the bags are stacked outside cabin doors, and the port that was once a strange point of departure is now a friendly welcome home.

The *Inquirer* nosed her way into Genoa, leaving the charms of Portofino severely unattainable to the east. Unnoticed by most of those who stood on deck and tried to fill in time before landing, a small launch put out into the bay and eventually came alongside to put on board a man who looked rather like an Italian version of an Inspector from Scotland Yard; which is what he was.

The monotony was broken by the voice of Burrows, tinnily disembodied over the loudspeakers.

"When we arrive at Genoa, all passengers are kindly requested to go to the main lounge to receive their passports. We hope you have enjoyed your cruise, and we wish you a pleasant journey home."

The voice faltered, as if choked with emotion at the thought of losing so many wonderful people. There was a rustle of paper and a whispered consultation, then the firm tones of Springer came over the loudspeakers:

"Inspector Montero's seen the Captain, and he says it's

all right, so you'd better get on with it, mate. And we want you down there too——"

The microphone was hastily switched off, while a murmur of amusement and conjectures floated around the deck. A few minutes later, the loudspeakers crackled and the voice of Burrows emerged again.

"Here is a further announcement about the collection of passports. The following passengers are kindly requested to go and receive their passports in the small writing-room: Mr. and Mrs. David Acton, Miss Theresa Acton...."

The list of names continued, while the murmur of voices on the deck grew louder.

Inspector Montero carefully closed the door of the writing-room. The windows looked out on the seaward side and gave the impression that they were still far from land. He went and sat behind one of the tables, taking a chair between Ludlow and a neat, dark man; he looked exactly as if he were the chairman at the meeting of some learned society. This impression was heightened when he spoke.

"Ladies and Gentlemen, this is Inspector Pellegrini of the Italian police. You all, I think, know Mr. Ludlow."

Pellegrini glared suspiciously at the audience and clasped his hands firmly over a little pile of passports which lay in front of him. Some of the audience glared back, while others looked out blankly to the freedom of the open sea beyond the windows.

The audience was small, but well representative of the crew and passengers of the *Inquirer*. Burrows sat near the door, looking pale and tired; perhaps from the burden of ending another cruise, perhaps not. Harmer, seeming dirtier and shabbier without his white steward's coat, stood with folded arms by the window. David and Elizabeth Acton did not take their eyes from the passports, the symbol of release that was being withheld. Theresa was leaning against one of the bookcases, looking bored and clinging to Rupert Penge. Her attachment seemed to suggest defiance rather than affection. Rupert himself was stern and tight-lipped, looking like a man who is trying to discover some rights that he can assert. The Grossheims sat a little away from the rest. Joseph, an older man than the one who had embarked on the cruise, continually wiped his face with a yellow silk handkerchief. Cornelia did not look at him, but sat twisting her hands in her lap as if performing some invisible and intricate embroidery. Julie West, clutching the bag which had been stolen and retrieved in Naples, sat and looked admiringly at Ludlow. Springer stood with his back to the door and contemplated the imitation panelling on the opposite wall.

"Mr. Ludlow would like to speak to us," Montero said, looking more like a chairman than ever.

"And suppose we don't want to listen to him? You can't make us stay here." It was David Acton, suddenly red in the face and aggressive.

"That is quite true, Mr. Acton. We are not numbered among the students, now far away, who are obliged to attend his lectures. The happier we, no doubt."

The Italian Inspector raised his eyes in silent protest against this extraordinary condescension towards a suspect. David got up, and beckoned to Elizabeth to do the same. Montero's mild blue eyes were steel-cold.

"You are free to leave the cabin now," he said. "But you will not leave the ship until your passport is returned to you. And that will be when I am ready, not before."

"'We have to catch the train for Milan, to make our connexion with the airport. We haven't got much time."

"Then the sooner we get started, the better. You will all catch your trains and planes—at least, most of you will."

David glared at him, then sat down heavily. Montero looked at Ludlow, who leaned forward across the table and looked as if he were about to deliver some interesting facts about the Elizabethan theatre. What he in fact said was quite different.

"During the last week or so, we have been living under conditions which are rare in the modern world. We have been members of a completely closed community, seeing each other every day and with our lives bounded for most of the time by the physical limitations of the ship. Even on shore, we have been herded together by the amiable sheep-dogs arranged by Mr. Burrows, while the shortness of time and difficulties of language have prevented us from making any real contact with the inhabitants of places which we have visited. For most of the year we are comparatively free to move where we wish, to choose our company at least for part of the time, and generally to avoid unpleasantness. We see it coming, so to speak, and step out of the way. It is salutary for us to experience a way of life similar to that which prevailed for the greater part of past history. People were born into a community, grew up and died in it. They knew each other intimately—the weaknesses, the follies, the dangers that lurk in every person. Seeing few strangers, they naturally attached supreme importance to their immediate circle. Our study of literature will be inadequate unless we can imaginatively enter into such a state of mind."

Some of the listeners were looking interested and almost ready to take notes, while others were becoming mutinous. Montero coughed and nudged Ludlow gently, but the instruction went on unchecked.

"In these conditions, it is inevitable that strains and tensions should build up. A young woman who might soon be forgotten in a busy town comes to be regarded as supremely desirable. A slight insult which would normally be shrugged off may smoulder into a grievance that bursts into the flame of hatred. A danger that could be easily escaped on shore may become a menace to survival at sea."

Ludlow paused and looked slowly at each of them in turn. Some met his gaze, some looked away. Pellegrini seemed to press down more heavily on the pile of passports in front of him.

"Some tension of this kind has grown up among us. The result has been two violent deaths: in fact, murder by poisoning. I should like you all to join me now in a quiet analysis of possibilities. Let us begin with the members of the staff—er, the crew—who no doubt will have duties to attend to and wish to get away as soon as possible. First, we have Harmer, the steward who prepared the tray on which the poisoned juice was found."

Harmer said, "I never——" then realized the implication of what Ludlow had just said about getting away. A smile spread over his face.

"Now Harmer," Ludlow went on, "had an excellent opportunity to put in the poison. He knew for whom he was preparing the tray, and he had already got on bad terms with Miss Acton. This might have been a wonderful opportunity to ensure that no complaint would be made against him at the end of the cruise. He would naturally want to continue in this job——"

"Don't you believe it," Harmer said. "I'm leaving this ship as soon as I'm paid off. She's unlucky—and I can soon get another berth at this time of the year."

"Quite so. That confirms what I have already decided. Both your own attitude to your job and the concern expressed by Mr. Burrows about getting suitable men made it unlikely that the disapproval of one passenger would incite you to murder. However, since you also had an excellent chance of poisoning the drink which killed Adrian Mallaby, it was necessary to keep you under suspicion a little longer. But now, you may go."

"Thanks very much," Harmer said nastily. "I'm staying to see the end of this."

"Anyone who wishes can stay, of course. Now we come to Mr. Burrows."

Harmer remained firmly in his place. Burrows looked as if he might order him to leave, but thought better of it and stared at Ludlow instead.

"Mr. Burrows was an interesting possibility," Ludlow went on, "because he was at the nerve-centre, as it were.

The various tensions and disagreements among the passengers would almost certainly be known to him. He had the opportunity of observing them and becoming familiar with their habits, without seeming to do more than his duty. He could know when cabins were likely to be empty and could have a reasonable excuse for being in almost any part of the ship. He could very easily have abstracted the poison which we now know was left in the cabin for some days and he could have put it into the jug while pretending to examine the tray. Further, he had had a bit of a scene with Miss Acton, over her cabin and over another matter which perhaps we need not now discuss. Unlike Harmer, he would be unwilling to risk losing his job and having to find a comparable one quickly."

"Look here, Ludlow, we don't need all this. Let's say you're clever, and leave it at that. Come to the point." It was David Acton, half on his feet again but subsiding under a look from Montero.

"You do me an injustice if you think I am trying to demonstrate any skill of my own," Ludlow said patiently. "After the close proximity in which we have lived, and the many suspicions that have been felt and indeed voiced among us, it is as well that the mystery should be solved clearly and unambiguously. There must be no lingering doubts, when we part."

There was a general murmur, which might have been either approval or disgust. Only Julie West, admiringly watching Ludlow, looked as if she might be about to applaud.

"To continue then," Ludlow said. "I will be as expeditious as truth allows. Mr. Burrows did not commit either of the murders."

"Who did then? Come to the point," David insisted.

"I will deal next with the case of Mr. David Acton, who seems to be particularly anxious to get things over."

"Do you wonder at it, man? After all, she was my sister——"

"Yes, indeed. And through her death you inherit a large

sum of money, which you confess to needing rather urgently. You stood to gain most by her death, and you perhaps could most easily approach her without her suspicion. When you left dinner on that evening, nothing could have been easier than to put poison in the jug which was still outside the door, take the tray in to your sister and watch her while she drank and died. Then you could be back in full view of the others long before her body was discovered. Indeed, if Miss West had not shown a kindly concern for her new friend and gone down immediately after dinner, it might have been much later. Then your movements would have faded from our memories, and you would no doubt have had a good alibi for the whole time after dinner."

"Look here, I've made a statement—I've told what happened——"

"But only after your fingerprints were discovered on the tray. Such carelessness can convict a man. But in this case, it made me inclined to elimate you from suspicion. Give Mr. Acton his passport, Inspector."

Pellegrini picked up a passport and showed it to Ludlow.

"Ah yes, I see. Mr. and Mrs. Acton travel on the same passport, so perhaps we had better withhold it for the moment. And, if you will allow me, I must now go into a slight digression."

"We'll be here all night at this rate," said Rupert Penge.

"Not all of us, I assure you. I have no intention of missing my train. Now, Inspector, when we looked at the cabin together, do you remember a remark I made as we were leaving?"

"You said something about it being rather phoney—yes, and you drew my attention to the telephone," Montero said.

"Quite so. Yes, one picks up a great deal of unfortunate slang in one's travels. Of course, in a sense it is slang which helps to keep the language alive and vigorous—however, on this occasion my choice of word was not accidental. The appearance of the telephone was significant. It had been put back on its rest in the way that would be easiest for a person holding it in the right hand. *But Diana Acton was left-handed.* We had abundant proof of this from her brother; and left-handed prints were found from the glass on the floor."

"This is absurd," said Rupert Penge, looking as if he could conduct a triumphant cross-examination. "Most people are pretty well ambidextrous as far as the telephone is concerned. I mean a right-handed person will hold the phone in the left hand if he wants to write——"

"But why should Miss Acton have wanted to write while she was asking for a tray to be sent down?"

"Well—the point wouldn't stand up for a moment in Court."

"I entirely agree. I never regarded it as evidence, only as opening an interesting line of thought. For if my conjecture was correct, there were two possibilities. Either someone used the phone after the order had been given, or Miss Acton never gave the order at all."

"But it was received in the pantry——" Burrows began.

"An order was received, certainly. But from whom? The Chief Steward naturally accepted it as coming from Miss Acton, and never claimed to recognize her voice. It was just the sort of voice that he would expect to hear from an English woman with a first-class cabin. And now, after that digression, we come to Mrs. Acton."

Elizabeth was pale, and clutched her husband's arm. For the first time since they had started, even Theresa showed anxiety under her sullen glare.

"Now Mrs. Acton," Ludlow went on, "profits by her husband's inheritance. We can understand, and no doubt feel sympathy for, the jealousy and dislike which she must have had for her sister-in-law. To be struggling for money that had been lost only by a whim of inheritance, to depend even for a holiday on grudging loans—what wonder if this should drive a woman to murder? What could be easier than to slip into the cabin, perhaps while Diana was having a shower, to telephone for a tray, to put in poison——"

Elizabeth was crying, and David was on his feet again. He leapt towards the table with clenched fists. Springer caught him in flight and firmly restored him to his place. Rupert Penge had to shout to be heard.

"But this is nonsense," he said. "If Diana herself didn't ask for the tray, she would simply have ignored it. Why didn't she come to dinner?"

"Perhaps because she was already dead."

"But then, how did she—I mean——"

"Be patient a little longer. Inspector, give Mr. and Mrs. Acton their passport."

David subsided with a gasp as the little book was handed to him.

"Miss Theresa Acton," Ludlow said, looking as if he might be about to ask her to read her essay. "A very foolish and immature young woman, I fear."

"What blasted cheek," said Theresa.

"Immature, I repeat, and therefore subject to that jealousy which the very young can feel for those still young but more sophisticated. When this jealousy is combined with the greed for money, it might well turn to hatred, and hatred to violence. Foolish, I repeat also, the height of her folly being in carrying a tin of deadly poison with her simply so as to look interesting and important. Or was it folly? Was it perhaps a cover for deadly intent? The way to avert suspicion may sometimes be to court it. For instance, Inspector, if you met a man in the street with a suspicious parcel, and he told you that he was carrying dynamite with which to blow up the Bank of England——"

"I should nick him at once, on suspicion," Montero said.

"Oh. However, we must next ask what happened to this tin of poison. First we are told that it had been thrown overboard, then that it had been mislaid. Perhaps it never left the possession of its original purchaser. Miss Theresa Acton was seen bending over the tray when it was outside her aunt's cabin. Suppose she herself had asked for it, pretending that the message came from her aunt——"

"Stop it!" Theresa jumped up, red-faced and without any veneer of sophistication left to cover her rage and humiliation. Rupert made encouraging noises and took her hand, but she pushed him away.

"Give the child her passport, since she is just old enough to have one in her own right. She has learnt her lesson," Ludlow said.

Theresa snatched her passport and, pushing past Springer, ran out of the cabin. Elizabeth rose to go after her, but David gently drew her back. Pellegrini studied the diminished pile of passports. The next two that he picked up, looking all the time at Ludlow, were green and clearly the property of United States citizens.

Now Mr. and Mrs. Grossheim," Ludlow said comfortably, "had built up their own particular tension around Miss Acton. We need not now consider the details of those foolish impulses which mankind will glorify into grand passions. In this case, they did not seem to be adequate grounds for murder, though violent death has come often enough out of emotions as slight as these. But I was given what we may call the American angle, when it seemed that Miss West was in danger, and that she had been planning some kind of financial deal with the dead woman. These were significant facts, though not quite in the way which I first thought of them, and which caused me to cast suspicion on Mr. and Mrs. Grossheim."

"This is an outrage," said Joseph P. Grossheim. "I want to see a lawyer."

"I doubt whether you would find one in Genoa suitable for your purpose, so that will have to wait. Just pay attention. As I was saying, I ceased to think of Mr. Grossheim as a specimen of angry American manhood rebuffed, and of his wife as an outraged pillar of the Revolution—or what do they call themselves? It seemed that deeper motives may have lain behind that romantic if brief encounter. When Mrs. Grossheim stayed down in her cabin during dinner, so that she could work destruction with the poison which her husband had abstracted from the cabin of——"

"Oh, Joe," wailed Cornelia.

"I'll sue you for defamation," Joseph shouted, "I'll sue the company for mental strain, I'll sue the police——"

"Give them their passports," Ludlow said.

The cabin was very quiet after Joseph Grossheim had sat down. Rupert Penge shifted uneasily and looked at the door.

"I think I'll go and see how Theresa's getting on," he said.

"Don't you want your passport?" Ludlow asked.

"I'll have it later—oh, all right, get on with it."

"Very well. Now, Rupert Penge, a barrister. Therefore a young man who has seen something of the criminal world and might have studied some useful methods——"

"I don't do much criminal work. I specialize in——"

"Don't interrupt. Here we have a young man who has also been rebuffed by Diana Acton, and in favour of the unsavoury Mallaby at that. But we learn also that he is ambitious and in need of money. If his new attachment to Theresa were to lead to marriage, at a time when her father had suddenly become rich, we might think that we had a good motive. Or was his attachment even more a matter of expediency: a way of making sure that Theresa did not give away something that she knew? After all, she was the owner of the poison which has caused all the trouble. It would be sad to see a promising career at the Bar cut short. Fortunately, it is not necessary. Let him have his passport."

There was silence again. Then David Acton laughed harshly.

"Well," he said, "where does that leave us? Was all this pantomime put on just to tell us that my sister's death remains an unsolved mystery?"

"You rush to conclusions too easily," Ludlow said. "So

far we have been concentrating on one murder only, and indeed there seems little proof that can fasten our suspicions on anyone. I decided next to work through the second murder, which seemed to be part of a plot of violence against Miss West. Presumably she knew something about the first murder, though without realizing it, and had to be removed. At this point suspicion was strong against Adrian Mallaby, who had apparently been much in the company of Diana Acton, and had been threatening and frightening her. When it turned out that he was a man with a criminal record, we seemed to have the answer. Miss Acton was keeping some very valuable jewellery in her cabin. That seemed to link up too."

"So Adrian Mallaby killed Diana for her jewels. But he didn't get them," Rupert Penge said.

"No, he didn't get them. Nevertheless, it did look very much as if the second poisoning had somehow removed our first murderer by accident. *But Mallaby was not killed by accident.*"

"But he drank out of my glass," Julie objected.

"Let me go on. When I came to study this second death, it seemed as if nobody could have put the poison in the drink. While the glasses were on the table, everybody was dancing. I know little about modern dancing and care less, but it does seem to me impossible that one partner could accurately drop something into a small glass on a table without the other one noticing. And the combination of couples on this occasion did not seem to produce much likelihood of conspiracy, though admittedly there were possibilities. But the fact remained that only one person had sat alone at that table from the time the drinks were brought until Mallaby returned. That person could easily have dropped in the poison while everyone else was occupied. For it was her safety that the police were then guarding, and at that time she seemed to be perfectly safe and not to need close watching."

All looked at Julie West, who was crimson with anger. She clutched her bag defiantly and waited.

"But wait a minute," said Grossheim, "are you trying to tell us that Julie poisoned her own drink?"

""Certainly not, though at first I was faced by that logical difficulty. But then I realized the absurdity of assuming that anyone else could have known which drink was meant for her and which for her companion. How could any of the dancers have chosen the right glass? How indeed did we know that the poisoned drink was hers? *Because she told us so.* She shouted it when Mallaby was already unable to speak, and we believed her. But in fact she had poisoned the drink which Mallaby had ordered for himself."

Julie looked quite calmly at Ludlow, and smiled.

"Why, Professor," she said, "you must be crazy. Why would I want to kill Adrian Mallaby?"

"Because he was blackmailing you with information that would point clearly to the fact that you killed Diana Acton."

"That's just ridiculous. I was with you on deck before the tray was even taken down to her cabin."

"By which time she was already dead."

"Are you saying that the orange juice was not poisoned?" David Acton asked.

"No, I am only saying that it did not kill her. As I thought back I realized how much depended on Miss West's unsupported word. For instance, that Mallaby was threatening Miss Acton; in fact, he was trying to exploit her and had every interest in keeping her alive. Then we believed that Miss Acton had not drunk anything during the afternoon when she and Miss West were on deck together. Some orange juice had in fact been ordered, but who had drunk it? Naturally, nobody had noticed that, in their quiet corner of the deck, Miss Acton had allowed it to be fetched by her companion, and had drunk it herself. Then they went to their cabin; Miss Acton prepared the sherry while Miss West was having a shower. All very reasonable, except that it happened the other way round. The sherry was prepared while Miss Acton was in the bathroom, a poisoned glass was given to her and she fell dead at once. Her murderer washed the glass, was careful to put a little fresh sherry at the bottom, telephoned to the pantry for a tray and then came to join me on deck."

"But it doesn't work," said Rupert Penge, "If she was killed then, how did she drink the orange juice?"

"She didn't. What was found in her stomach was orange juice—which of course she had drunk on deck—sherry and cyanide. Since poisoned orange juice was found in her cabin, it was assumed that she had drunk some of it. In fact, what happened was this. Miss West hurried down to the cabin after dinner, put cyanide in the jug and wiped the tray and jug clean of fingerprints. She omitted to wipe underneath, where Mr. Acton had held it. She then poured out and disposed of a glassful of juice, pressed Miss Acton's left hand on the empty glass and ran back to give the alarm."

"That's a pretty story, Professor," said Julie, "but you just try and prove it."

Montero turned to the Italian Inspector, who had been trying to follow the proceedings and was looking rather lost.

"You have the report from Naples, Inspector Pellegrini?"

He took the sheet of paper which was handed to him.

"We know all about yesterday's episode," he said. "The man who was hired to steal your bag has blown the whole story. The Naples police have got Favillo. Miss West, will you please give me your handbag?"

"No, I will not. Who is this guy Favillo? And what do you expect to find in my bag? Maybe you think it's stuffed full of cyanide."

"I'm sure you've already disposed of that. I just want to see your passport."

"What do you mean? You have my passport, right there on the table."

Montero suddenly leaned over and seized Julie's bag with as much skill as the Neapolitan thief had shown.

"Give that back," Julie exclaimed.

Montero opened the bag and extracted a blue British passport. He looked at the front cover. "Jane Waters," he said. "As I told you, Mr. Ludlow, they usually keep the same initials."

"I think we're entitled to some explanation," said David Acton.

"You'll get it in the reports of the trial, sir. Now, Miss West, or Miss Waters, I am going to take you back to London, where you will be charged with the wilful murder of Diana Acton. You are not obligated to say anything, but I have to warn you that anything you say will be taken down and may be given in evidence."

"Damn you," said Julie in an unmistakably English voice.

Ludlow did not look at her when he got up and went to the door.

"I've got to catch my train," he said. "I'll see you in London, Inspector."

— 16 —

"It has truly been said that the British and American peoples are separated only by the barrier of a common language," said Ludlow.

A week after disembarking from the *Inquirer,* he was sitting with Montero in a pub near Scotland Yard. Outside, the English summer was asserting itself in bursts of wind and rain.

"Yes," he continued, "Jane Waters really did very well in her assumed role of Julie West. But during the first days of the cruise, she hadn't fully mastered the idiom. Now I do not subscribe to the belief held by some people in this country that the Americans speak a kind of slang version of English. Still, there are differences. An American, although seemingly always in a hurry, prefers the four syllables of *elevator* to the single one of *lift*—this being one of the differences of vocabulary which our friend had not mastered. When she referred to Diana Acton as *homely,* I knew that she was not an American; for that unhappy woman was certainly far from plain or ugly. Then there are differences of syntax. At one point Julie—I suppose I might as well call her that even now—used the phrase *haven't got,* where an American would have certainly said *don't have.* This variation raises an interesting point of historical grammar——"

"All right," Montero broke in. "I get the idea. You knew she wasn't an American and quite rightly suspected that she was acting a part for no good purpose. Wait till I've got some more to drink and then tell me all."

When this mission had been accomplished, Ludlow lit his pipe and settled into what his students would have recognized as a comfortable tutorial attitude.

"As I explained on the ship," he said, "I soon realized that much of our evidence depended on her unsupported word—even to the fact that Diana had decided to stay in her cabin and ring for a tray. It was not until I understood the significance of the jewels that I knew what her motive was. She was threatened with exposure, so she killed twice, brutally and cold-bloodedly, to keep herself out of prison. Am I right? Fill me in, as they say nowadays."

"Quite right," said Montero. "She's an international jewel-thief and confidence trickster. In the late Mallaby's line of business, but with rather better criminal connexions. She's refused to make any statement, but we've got all we want from our own records and from Interpol. She's never actually been convicted, but she's known under a good many names and disguises."

"And of course this famous American property company is fictitious."

"Oh no, the company's genuine enough. You remember that Diana checked up on that with her solicitors. The fictitious part was Julie West's share in it. That was just the softening-up process. She didn't want any money invested in it—that would have done her no good at all. It was the lead towards getting the jewellery, which was her special line. Most criminals have one."

"I'd never have pieced it all together without your help," Ludlow said magnanimously. "It was when you were talking about some of the methods of confidence tricksters that I realized what she was really after. In a variation on the wallet trick, they were to pool their jewels—one lot, of course, being worthless. But then Adrian Mallaby recognized her."

"Yes, everything was set for her success. It was her misfortune that the same cruise was being worked by a crook who knew her, and who had no conception of what's amusingly known as honour among thieves—there isn't much, you know. Everything had gone smoothly, even to the change of cabin, which was a stroke of luck, until Mallaby started suggesting that his silence would be worth paying for. Being a young criminal of some spirit, she refused to play. Then, as you yourself were able to see, he started hanging round Diana."

"Yes, that unlikely attachment puzzled a lot of people, not least Rupert Penge. When Mallaby was dead and revealed for what he was, it was easy for Julie West to persuade us that he had been threatening Diana and must have had some kind of a hold over her. In fact, of course, he was telling her all about her new friend, and no doubt hoping to profit by working one of his own tricks after gaining her confidence in that way. Julie spent the afternoon before the murder in trying to persuade her to change her mind and keep quiet. Diana must have told her what she had found out, and also perhaps that she had arranged to tell the Captain that very evening."

"In that case, she couldn't have planned it much in advance."

"'No, I don't think she did. Perhaps the exact method didn't occur to her until Diana drank some orange juice—a fact which it was quite easy to conceal from us later."

"The pathologist's report was positive that it had been drunk some time before death," Montero said. "We'd never have got her on that alone, especially as the ship's doctor was neither very prompt nor efficient in removing the contents of the stomach."

"Still, it gave her the chance she wanted. She saw that Diana was adamant, so pretended to acquiesce in the situation and have no hard feelings. Certainly she joined Diana in a glass of sherry—and the rest of her actions were as we know. She must have secreted the tin of poison early in the afternoon, as soon as she had a warning that it might be needed. Theresa went to look for it later and couldn't find it, so Julie probably had it in that famous and capacious bag of hers."

"She didn't make many mistakes, you know," Montero

said thoughtfully. She wiped the tray and the jug too clean, forgetting that they ought to have had Diana's prints on them. But that only showed that someone had handled them and tried to hide the fact; it didn't point to her at all. The telephone call would actually point away from her, if we ever came to suspect that it wasn't Diana who made it. She used her natural English voice, and that put suspicion on somebody like Elizabeth Acton. And there was just the right amount of orange juice in the stomach and the right amount gone from the jug. Yes, she was smart all right."

A cold draught wandered into the bar and crept around their legs. The rain outside beat on the window, threatening the end of permitted hours and the need for emergence into the night. It may have been this thought which made Ludlow shiver slightly, or it may have been something quite different.

"But she couldn't stop at one murder," Montero said. "Mallaby became more pressing than ever. If she were exposed now for what she was, the suspicion of murder would fall on her very strongly. No doubt he raised the price of his silence considerably. So she made us believe that she feared an attack, actually made us watch her closely and then got away with murder under our noses. Simple enough, but those are the most difficult to solve. To think that I was actually afraid she might get into some trouble if I let her go on shore at Naples."

"I was quite sure that she would," Ludlow said, "but it would be planned trouble. She had to dispose of the jewellery somehow, and she could hardly walk off with it at the end of the cruise. The change in her plans came as soon as she had done the first murder. The jewellery was in your custody and it was important that the false stuff with it shouldn't be traced to her. However, when all communications to and from the ship were presumably being checked by you, she dared not get in touch with her accomplices at Naples. She had to let the arrangement go through—but you haven't told me the end of that part."

"The Naples police soon got the story. The actual thief was working for one of the biggest crooks in the city, to whom he was supposed to deliver the bag and its contents. The woman from whose hand he was to grab it had been accurately described to him. His big surprise came when he found a British copper on his heels. No sooner had the strains of 'Rule Britannia' died down than his boss got *his* big surprise by a visit from the local equivalent of the C.I.D. We seem to have broken up a profitable little business down there, and one which has links in other parts of Europe. Oh yes, our Julie was in high-class stuff."

"As I said, your information about methods made it quite clear. The jewellery was to be carried on shore with some pretext—probably the old trick of showing confidence in each other. Perhaps Diana would have been entrusted with the false stuff. Then the bag containing her jewels would have been snatched, disappearing down an alley with no blame attached to Julie. She remained an innocent victim, and collected her share later."

"Now, your last orders, please." The dismal shout broke the silence into which both men had fallen.

"This is a most inhospitable country," Ludlow said. "In Italy, we could now be sitting out under the stars, drinking wine at leisure and going on with our conversation."

"You're welcome to sit outside here for as long as you like. Same?"

"It's my turn."

"No, I insist. This case is giving me a good lot of credit, which I have to owe partly to you."

Ten minutes later, Ludlow knocked out his pipe, got up and began to button his indescribable raincoat.

"This really is an abominable climate," he said. "I'm sure all those atoms they let off are responsible for it."

"Maybe. Anyway, I'm on holiday from Saturday, so let's hope it clears up."

"Are you going abroad?" Ludlow asked as they braced themselves for their final plunge into the street.

"No fear. I'm going to Devon, my native county and the

fairest place on earth. I'll send you some cream."

The Inspector disappeared towards the Embankment, and Ludlow made his way up Northumberland Avenue against the wind. The traffic swished wetly past, but what he seemed to hear were different sounds. There was the wash of the sea against a ship that ploughed along in the sunshine; and there were confused voices, some of them uttering their own doom.

THE PERENNIAL LIBRARY MYSTERY SERIES

Ted Allbeury

THE OTHER SIDE OF SILENCE	P 669, $2.84
PALOMINO BLONDE	P 670, $2.84
SNOWBALL	P 671, $2.84

Delano Ames

CORPSE DIPLOMATIQUE	P 637, $2.84
FOR OLD CRIME'S SAKE	P 629, $2.84
MURDER, MAESTRO, PLEASE	P 630, $2.84
SHE SHALL HAVE MURDER	P 638, $2.84

E. C. Bentley

TRENT'S LAST CASE	P 440, $2.50
TRENT'S OWN CASE	P 516, $2.25

Andrew Bergman

THE BIG KISS-OFF OF 1944	P 673, $2.84
HOLLYWOOD AND LEVINE	P 674, $2.84

Gavin Black

A DRAGON FOR CHRISTMAS	P 473, $1.95
THE EYES AROUND ME	P 485, $1.95
YOU WANT TO DIE, JOHNNY?	P 472, $1.95

Nicholas Blake

THE CORPSE IN THE SNOWMAN	P 427, $1.95
END OF CHAPTER	P 397, $1.95
HEAD OF A TRAVELER	P 398, $2.25
MINUTE FOR MURDER	P 419, $1.95
THE MORNING AFTER DEATH	P 520, $1.95
A PENKNIFE IN MY HEART	P 521, $2.25

Lionel Davidson

THE MENORAH MEN	P 592, $2.84
NIGHT OF WENCESLAS	P 595, $2.84
THE ROSE OF TIBET	P 593, $2.84

D. M. Devine

MY BROTHER'S KILLER	P 558, $2.40

Kenneth Fearing

THE BIG CLOCK	P 500, $1.95

Andrew Garve

THE ASHES OF LODA	P 430, $1.50
THE CUCKOO LINE AFFAIR	P 451, $1.95
A HERO FOR LEANDA	P 429, $1.50
MURDER THROUGH THE LOOKING GLASS	P 449, $1.95
NO TEARS FOR HILDA	P 441, $1.95
THE RIDDLE OF SAMSON	P 450, $1.95

Michael Gilbert

BLOOD AND JUDGMENT	P 446, $1.95
THE BODY OF A GIRL	P 459, $1.95
FEAR TO TREAD	P 458, $1.95

Joe Gores

HAMMETT	P 631, $2.84

C. W. Grafton

BEYOND A REASONABLE DOUBT	P 519, $1.95
THE RAT BEGAN TO GNAW THE ROPE	P 639, $2.84

Edward Grierson

THE SECOND MAN	P 528, $2.25

Bruce Hamilton

TOO MUCH OF WATER P 635, $2.84

Cyril Hare

DEATH IS NO SPORTSMAN P 555, $2.40

DEATH WALKS THE WOODS P 556, $2.40

AN ENGLISH MURDER P 455, $2.50

SUICIDE EXCEPTED P 636, $2.84

TENANT FOR DEATH P 570, $2.84

TRAGEDY AT LAW P 522, $2.25

UNTIMELY DEATH P 514, $2.25

THE WIND BLOWS DEATH P 589, $2.84

WITH A BARE BODKIN P 523, $2.25

Robert Harling

THE ENORMOUS SHADOW P 545, $2.50

Matthew Head

THE CABINDA AFFAIR P 541, $2.25

THE CONGO VENUS P 597, $2.84

MURDER AT THE FLEA CLUB P 542, $2.50

M. V. Heberden

ENGAGED TO MURDER P 533, $2.25

James Hilton

WAS IT MURDER? P 501, $1.95

S. B. Hough

DEAR DAUGHTER DEAD P 661, $2.84

SWEET SISTER SEDUCED P 662, $2.84

P. M. Hubbard

HIGH TIDE P 571, $2.40

Elspeth Huxley

THE AFRICAN POISON MURDERS	P 540, $2.25
MURDER ON SAFARI	P 587, $2.84

Francis Iles

BEFORE THE FACT	P 517, $2.50
MALICE AFORETHOUGHT	P 532, $1.95

Michael Innes

APPLEBY ON ARARAT	P 648, $2.84
APPLEBY'S END	P 649, $2.84
THE CASE OF THE JOURNEYING BOY	P 632, $3.12
DEATH ON A QUIET DAY	P 677, $2.84
DEATH BY WATER	P 574, $2.40
HARE SITTING UP	P 590, $2.84
THE LONG FAREWELL	P 575, $2.40
THE MAN FROM THE SEA	P 591, $2.84
ONE MAN SHOW	P 672, $2.84
THE SECRET VANGUARD	P 584, $2.84
THE WEIGHT OF THE EVIDENCE	P 633, $2.84

Mary Kelly

THE SPOILT KILL	P 565, $2.40

Lange Lewis

THE BIRTHDAY MURDER	P 518, $1.95

Allan MacKinnon

HOUSE OF DARKNESS	P 582, $2.84

Frank Parrish

FIRE IN THE BARLEY	P 651, $2.84
SNARE IN THE DARK	P 650, $2.84
STING OF THE HONEYBEE	P 652, $2.84

Austin Ripley

MINUTE MYSTERIES P 387, $2.50

Thomas Sterling

THE EVIL OF THE DAY P 529, $2.50

Julian Symons

THE BELTING INHERITANCE P 468, $1.95

BOGUE'S FORTUNE P 481, $1.95

THE COLOR OF MURDER P 461, $1.95

Dorothy Stockbridge Tillet
(John Stephen Strange)

THE MAN WHO KILLED FORTESCUE P 536, $2.25

Simon Troy

THE ROAD TO RHUINE P 583, $2.84

SWIFT TO ITS CLOSE P 546, $2.40

Henry Wade

THE DUKE OF YORK'S STEPS P 588, $2.84

A DYING FALL P 543, $2.50

THE HANGING CAPTAIN P 548, $2.50

Hillary Waugh

LAST SEEN WEARING . . . P 552, $2.40

THE MISSING MAN P 553, $2.40

Henry Kitchell Webster

WHO IS THE NEXT? P 539, $2.25

John Welcome

GO FOR BROKE P 663, $2.84

RUN FOR COVER P 664, $2.84

STOP AT NOTHING P 665, $2.84